She war
this child.

There was no way Caralie intended to forget the issue of custody. But she also needed to find out what had happened to her sister.

As she followed Riley into his house, Caralie wondered if agreeing to stay with him was a mistake.

Something about him drew her...the dark mystery in his eyes, the appeal of his handsome features.

The one thing she couldn't afford to do was be seduced by him, but it was the one thing she couldn't resist....

Dear Reader,

Three of your favorite Intrigue writers have joined together to bring you this special, *brand-new* Lost & Found trilogy.

Three women go into labor in the same Texas hospital, and shortly after the babies are born, fire erupts. Though each mother and baby make it to safety, there's more than the mystery of birth to solve now....

This month Carla Cassidy concludes this extra-special trilogy with *A Father's Love.* In case you missed the previous two titles—Amanda Stevens's *Somebody's Baby* or B.J. Daniels's *A Father for Her Baby*—you can order them through the Harlequin Reader Service. In the U.S.: 3010 Walden Avenue, Buffalo, NY 14269; in Canada: P.O. Box 609, Fort Erie, Ontario, L2A 5X3. Send a check or money order for $3.99 (plus 75¢ postage) in the U.S. or $4.50 (plus $1.00 postage) in Canada for each book ordered.

We hope you've enjoyed Lost & Found!

Happy reading!

Debra Matteucci
Senior Editor & Editorial Coordinator
Harlequin Books
300 East 42nd Street
New York, NY 10017

A Father's Love

Carla Cassidy

TORONTO • NEW YORK • LONDON
AMSTERDAM • PARIS • SYDNEY • HAMBURG
STOCKHOLM • ATHENS • TOKYO • MILAN • MADRID
PRAGUE • WARSAW • BUDAPEST • AUCKLAND

ISBN 0-373-22498-2

A FATHER'S LOVE

This edition published by arrangement with Harlequin Books S.A.

Printed in U.S.A.

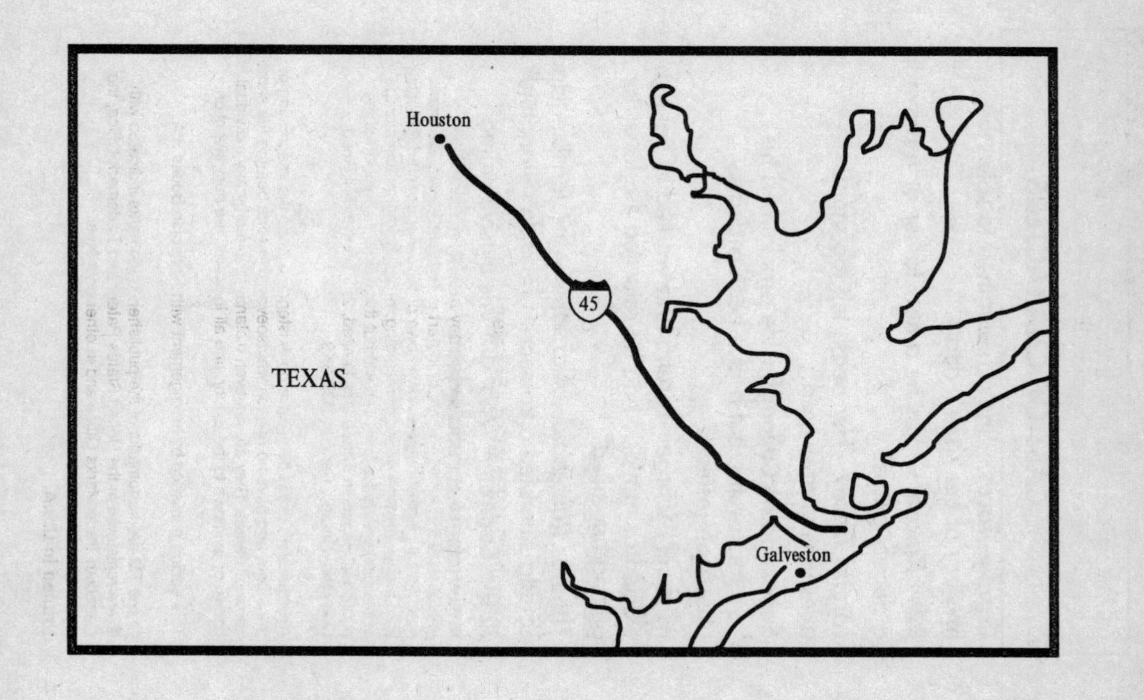
Houston
45
TEXAS
Galveston

CAST OF CHARACTERS

Caralie Tracey—She's determined to solve the mystery of her sister's death.

Riley Kincaid—Was he a new father or a pawn in a deadly game?

Loretta Tracey—Her death left too many questions unanswered.

Sebastian McCullough—He proclaimed his love for Loretta, but had it been a deadly obsession instead?

Michael Monroe—Loretta had worked to get him elected as mayor...had he returned the favor by getting her killed?

Thomas Rhinehold—Aka Tommy the Terrible. Had Loretta stumbled onto secrets he didn't want told?

Paula Cantrell—What did this elusive woman know about Loretta's death?

Chapter One

Children and animals. He'd been warned early in his career to steer clear of both. And for years he'd managed to do just that.

He'd been in Baghdad when the air strikes had lit up the sky like the Fourth of July, had snapped compelling photos of flood victims in North Dakota. Disasters, both natural and man-made, had kept him chasing from one end of the globe to the other, armed only with his trusty camera and a pad and pencil.

Riley Kincaid moved his camera tripod closer to the woman and dog who sat on a wing chair in front of a bright red heart-shaped backdrop.

The last place Riley wanted to be on the day after Christmas was in his studio taking Valentine's Day portrait photos of an old woman and her dog, but Winifred Bakerston had insisted she wanted the pictures taken today, and she was one of his best clients.

He'd heard that after years of cohabitation, pet owners began to take on the physical characteristics of their charges. Winifred and her bulldog, Sir Henry, proved the old wives' tale admirably.

''Mr. Kincaid, I believe Sir Henry is tiring.'' Winifred Bakerston's jowls flapped with impatience as she stroked the broad back of the drooling dog. ''He's quite high-strung, you know.''

Sir Henry was as high-strung as a boulder, Riley thought. ''Just a couple more shots,'' he said aloud. He smiled with as much charm as he could muster. ''After all, we want the absolute best picture we can get of you and Sir Henry. It's going to make a marvelous Valentine's Day photo—one that will last a lifetime.''

Winifred smiled, apparently pacified by the notion of a photo for posterity of her and her companion. ''Another few minutes, sweetheart,'' she said to the dog, who simply snorted his reply.

Riley snapped a last series of shots, eager to get the job done before Kaycee woke up demanding her lunch. He cast a quick glance toward the playpen in the corner, where a dark-haired, pink-clad baby slept peacefully, one thumb planted firmly in her rosebud mouth. His heart expanded with love.

Wouldn't his old buddies laugh long and hard if they could see him now? Wild Man Riley, tamed eight months ago by a six-pound eight-ounce delivery.

The bell hanging above the front door of the studio tinkled, indicating somebody had entered the front reception area. ''Excuse me for just a moment,'' he said to Winifred.

He had no other appointments for the day and assumed it was probably a day-after-Christmas-sale-shopper who'd wandered in by mistake. He left the studio area and entered the much smaller reception room.

A petite, dark-haired woman stood just inside the front door. In her attractive, though slightly exotic features, Riley found a strange, haunting familiarity, but he knew with certainty he'd never met or seen this woman before.

"Can I help you?" he asked.

"Riley Kincaid?" Her voice was low and melodic.

He nodded. "Yes, that's me."

She stepped forward, bringing with her the sensual fragrance of fresh-blooming flowers and mysterious spices. "I'm Caralie Tracey. I'm here about Loretta. I'm her sister."

Riley's head reeled with confusion and surprise. Loretta's sister? He took a step backward as his brain worked to make the connection. "I—I didn't know Loretta had any family," he finally managed to utter.

"She does. And I'm it," the woman said succinctly.

Riley stared back at her, realizing now why her features looked familiar. She had the same slight almond-shaped tilt to her blue-gray eyes, the same heart-shaped face and full lips as Loretta.

Loretta. It was the name of the woman who had forever changed Riley's life, the woman who had died nearly eight months before, just hours after having given birth to his daughter.

Riley's neat, packaged world—the world he had worked so hard to create—suddenly tilted askew. Why was she here? What did she want? And where in the hell had she been for the past seven months?

"Mr. Kincaid?" Winifred bustled out of the studio, the huge bulldog in her capable arms. "I'm afraid we'll have to finish the sitting another day. It's time for Sir Henry's lunch and he gets so upset when his schedule changes."

Riley drew a deep breath, attempting to slough off his shock. "I don't think we'll need another sitting," he said as he forced a smile at the matron and her slobbering pooch. "I'll call you when the proofs are ready and we'll set up a time to go over them."

It wasn't until Winifred Bakerston and Sir Henry had left that Riley could refocus his attention on Caralie Tracey. "You—uh—you said you're here about Loretta? I'm not sure I understand. What about her?"

The woman pulled her coat closer around her neck and sank into one of the waiting-room chairs. "I don't even know where to begin." She swept a hand through her long dark hair, her frown doing nothing to steal from her attractiveness.

"I've been out of the country for the past two years, working as a nurse's aide and teacher in small villages in Africa. Although Loretta and I tried to keep in touch, I only received mail about once every other month or so, whenever it could catch up to where we were. That's why I didn't know—wasn't here—" She broke off as her voice wavered with emotion.

Sympathy rose in Riley. How terrible, to find out nearly seven months after the fact that your sister had perished in a tragic inexplicable hospital fire. He shifted from foot to foot, not knowing what to do, how to comfort her.

Before he had a chance to say or do anything, a squeal emanated from the studio. Despite the awkward circumstances, Riley smiled. Kaycee had awakened, and the little girl never cried, but instead always squealed for attention the moment her eyes opened.

Caralie looked at Riley questioningly. "Is that..."

"My daughter." Riley was aware of the possessiveness of those words and for the first time he realized that Caralie's existence might change the neat and orderly world he'd built around his daughter.

"Loretta's child."

And in those two words, she challenged him with a truth he couldn't deny. Kaycee squealed again, demanding immediate attention. "I need to get her." He hesitated for a moment. "Come on in and meet your niece," he added.

She followed him into the studio, and he heard her swift intake of breath as she spied the dark-haired sprite who'd pulled herself up and now stood in the playpen grinning at them.

"Da-da, da-da." Kaycee bounced with excitement, displaying the two bottom teeth that had appeared in the past week.

"You want to get her out?" he asked grudgingly.

Caralie blinked, hesitated, then nodded. Riley watched her as she approached the playpen. Kaycee, an uncommonly pretty child, had never met a stranger she didn't like, and Caralie was no exception. Kaycee cooed in delight as Caralie picked her up.

Seeing the two together, it was impossible to miss

the physical similarities of their features. People had always commented that with her dark hair and the dimple that danced in one cheek, Kaycee looked like Riley. But as he saw the child and Caralie together, he realized all those people had been wrong. Kaycee's features were a miniature of her aunt's.

"What's her name?" Caralie asked.

Riley frowned, noting the way Caralie held Kaycee awkwardly, away from her body as if afraid the child might drool or spit up on her. In that instant, Riley decided he didn't much like Caralie Tracey.

"Her name is Katherine Tracey Kincaid. I call her Kaycee," he replied.

Caralie nodded and held the baby toward him. He took Kaycee, hugging her close to his chest as he stroked her silky dark hair. "She's ready for her lunch," he explained. "My place is upstairs—if you want to come up while she eats."

"Okay," Caralie replied.

It took Riley only a moment to lock up the studio, then Caralie followed him up the flight of stairs that led to his second-story apartment.

Riley's initial shock had worn off, taking with it some of the disquiet that had momentarily crept over him. It was only natural that Caralie would want to see her niece; it didn't mean the woman intended to disrupt his life.

It was just that Kaycee's birth had been such a surprise and Loretta's tragic death had been shrouded in mystery. No wonder he felt off-center at the sudden appearance of a sister he hadn't known existed.

"Take off your coat and come on into the

kitchen,'' he said as he led her through the living room. He was grateful he'd picked up the discarded Christmas wrappings and tidied the place late last night after his mother had gone home and Kaycee had been sleeping. The lights on the artificial Christmas tree in one corner still glowed and twinkled, giving the entire room a warm, cheerful aura.

In the kitchen, he placed Kaycee in her high chair and motioned Caralie into a chair at the table. ''On the menu today is Kaycee's favorite—hot dogs. Would you care for one?'' he asked as he opened the refrigerator door.

She smiled—the first full-blown one he'd seen from her. It lit up her features and reminded Riley that since Kaycee's appearance in his life he'd been living like a monk. He didn't have to like Caralie to find her physically attractive. ''No thanks, I already ate lunch,'' she replied.

It took him only a few moments to prepare a plate for Kaycee, complete with tiny pieces of cut-up hot dog, green peas and banana slices. He set the plate in front of Kaycee, who clapped her hands in delight at the sight of her favorite foods.

She grinned at Riley and he grinned back at her, wondering what he had done so right in his life to have been given this miracle child. He looked over at Caralie, who appeared utterly unmoved by the cute little girl. Cold. The woman was definitely cold.

As Kaycee began decimating her lunch, Riley sank into the chair opposite Caralie, unsure exactly what to say to her.

''I received the latest batch of letters from Loretta

two days ago and immediately got on a plane to come back here.'' Caralie laced her fingers together on the tabletop, her gaze downcast. ''I went to her apartment and found somebody else living there. They were the ones who told me Loretta was dead…had died in a hospital fire. I went to the Houston hospital and it was one of the administrators there who told me about the baby and that you had come to the hospital to claim her.''

She looked up at Riley, her eyes radiating grief. She drew a deep breath and the grief disappeared, was replaced by a grim determination. ''Tell me what you know about the fire. Tell me everything you know about Loretta. I need to somehow make sense of all this.''

Riley shrugged helplessly. ''There's not a lot I can tell you. Loretta and I didn't date for long.'' A flush warmed his cheeks as he thought of those crazy couple of weeks he'd spent with Loretta. She had been gorgeous and wild and sexy, but their brief affair had sputtered out as quickly as it had come to life.

''But you knew her well enough for her to become pregnant.'' He thought he sensed a touch of coolness in Caralie's tone.

Riley nodded. ''But at the time we stopped seeing each other I didn't have any idea she was pregnant with my child.'' He leaned forward. ''Look, I can't tell you much about Loretta's life in the months before the fire. She called me a day before Kaycee was born to tell me she was about to give birth to my child. That's the first I knew about the pregnancy.''

''In Loretta's letter where she told me she was

pregnant, she also indicated she knew the father wouldn't want the baby.'' There was no mistaking the coldness in her voice with this statement.

Riley frowned, uncomfortable with this foray into the past. He raked a hand through his hair and leaned back again. ''Sure, when Loretta and I were dating, we talked hypothetically about kids and I told her I wasn't ready to become a dad.''

He looked at Kaycee, who grinned back at him, her mouth decorated with mushed green peas and banana. ''But then 'hypothetical' became reality and everything changed.''

''Ga-ga,'' Kaycee babbled and held her arms out to Riley, her mouth pursed into a semi-pucker. He laughed and leaned forward, allowing the little girl to give him a sloppy kiss.

''Ga-ga,'' she repeated, her gaze turned toward Caralie.

''Uh—she wants to give you a kiss,'' Riley explained.

Caralie frowned, as if she found the idea distasteful, and again, dislike for her winged through Riley. Any idea he had of a loving, caring newfound aunt for Kaycee flew right out the window.

She leaned toward Kaycee, offering a cheek to the little girl, who smacked it happily, then held out a piece of hot dog to Caralie. Caralie shook her head, smiled curtly, then refocused her attention on Riley. ''You said Loretta called you the night before she died. How did she sound?''

Riley shrugged. ''I don't know.... She sounded nervous, anxious. I guess she sounded like a woman confessing to a man that she was about to have his baby and wasn't sure how he'd react.'' For a moment, sympathy swept through Riley—sympathy for this woman who so obviously needed to make sense of her sister's death. ''Look, I know this has all been a shock to you, but Loretta's death was one of life's tragic accidents that makes no sense.''

''I think you're wrong, Mr. Kincaid. I don't think it was a tragic accident at all,'' she replied, her voice shaking with suppressed emotion. ''I think Loretta was murdered.''

CARALIE WATCHED AS HIS mouth fell open and he gazed at her dumbly. She'd shocked him. Good. She'd suffered a series of shocks in the past twenty-four hours—the first in discovering Loretta was dead, and the last, when she'd realized the infamous Riley Kincaid was the father of Loretta's baby.

''That's crazy,'' he protested.

''From what little I've learned so far, investigators never found the cause of the fire at the hospital, and the case has never been closed.''

''That doesn't mean it was set intentionally to kill Loretta!'' he exclaimed. He stood and went to the sink for a glass of water, as if finding her words difficult to swallow without a little help.

She waited patiently for him to finish his drink. He was far more handsome than she'd anticipated. She'd expected him to look desiccated, old beyond his age from his years of living life in the fast lane. Loretta had always managed to get involved with men who were at least as dysfunctional as she was.

Loretta. Pain ripped through Caralie as she thought of her sister. Gone. Gone forever. No more opportunities for apologies, no more chances to reach for the dreams they'd planned together as two lonely little girls.

She consciously kept her gaze away from Loretta's daughter, the baby girl who so resembled her mother. Caralie actually wanted to bundle Kaycee into her arms, hug her tightly against her heart and never let her go, but she knew it would be her undoing. She had to maintain control over her emotions until she got some answers about Loretta's death.

She blinked and stuffed the grief away to suffer later. She didn't have time now—at the moment, there were other pressing matters.

Riley returned to the table, his gaze dark as he eyed her. "Why on earth would you think Loretta was murdered? Who would want to kill her?" he asked.

"I don't know who—but I intend to find out. Loretta was scared, frightened for her life." Caralie opened her purse and withdrew the letter that had prompted her immediate return to the States. "I received this three days ago. It's postmarked a week before Loretta gave birth."

He took it from her and read it silently. As he read, she studied him. Neatly cut, his dark hair had just enough curl to be attractive. His nose was straight, his mouth sensually full. His clothes—jeans and a long-sleeved shirt—were casual, but tasteful. Overall, he emitted an aura of confidence and stability. A different kind of man than she'd expected, judging by the stories she'd heard about him over the years.

There was something about him that stirred a powerful awareness in her. She'd forgotten what it was like to be attracted to a man on a purely physical level, and that was what Riley did.

How on earth had he hooked up with Loretta, who'd had a penchant for long-haired, tattooed ex-cons who made no promises, and for married men with double lives who'd made false ones? Granted, Riley Kincaid had a reputation for partying hard and living dangerously, but he was a cut above Loretta's usual choice in men.

He set the letter down, his eyes dark and enigmatic as he frowned at her. "Okay, so she wrote that she was in danger, that she was frightened about something and somebody, but you know your sister had a flair for drama." He shifted in his chair, as if uncomfortable with the idea of speaking ill of the dead.

"I'm well aware of Loretta's faults," she replied as she took the letter back from him. It had been Loretta's faults that had caused Caralie to pack up and leave, in an attempt to make her older sister grow up and become responsible. Again pain tore through Caralie, pain that mingled with an overwhelming guilt.

"But this doesn't read like manufactured drama," she continued as she folded the letter and placed it back in the envelope. "Don't you find it odd that three days before her death, she feared that something horrible would happen to her? She specifically says she knows she's in danger...that she knows too much.''

Kaycee babbled and pushed her plate aside. With the ease of practice, Riley caught the colorful plastic plate before it could skid off the tray and onto the floor. ''But she doesn't name names or mention anything specific. Knows too much about what?'' He shook his head. ''The fire and her death were just one of life's crazy, tragic coincidences,'' he said as he carried the plate to the sink, then returned with a wet cloth.

''I don't believe in those kinds of coincidences,'' Caralie replied.

He cleaned Kaycee's face and hands, then lifted the little girl into his arms. ''If you'll excuse me for a minute, I need to change her.''

''Bye-bye,'' Kaycee said to Caralie and again Caralie fought the urge to reach for the little girl and bury her face in Kaycee's dark hair, smell the wonderful innocence of babyhood.

''Bye-bye,'' Caralie responded, fighting to control her emotions.

Riley left the kitchen, leaving Caralie alone with her thoughts—frightening thoughts. She knew somebody had intentionally killed Loretta; she knew it in her gut. She planned to investigate and had hoped for Riley's help.

She stood and drifted from the kitchen into the living room. The Christmas tree sparkling in the corner sharpened the edge of grief that tried to take hold of her. Christmas—a time for family, for making memories. But this Christmas had brought only anguish.

She turned her head to gaze at the framed photos on the walls. Pictures of foreign people in distant places filled one, the other wall space was devoted to photos of Kaycee.

She studied the images of her niece first, her heart carefully and tightly restricted from feeling anything. She'd learned to control her emotions a long time ago—a survival instinct acquired while young and perfected more recently while working with the children in Africa.

She'd learned not to love too deeply or too intensely, because people often didn't love you back, or they disappeared...or died.

The pictures on the other wall were all familiar to her—photos she'd seen in newspapers and magazines at one time or another. Riley's personal life had been as colorful and newsworthy as his work, often garnering articles depicting a man who lived hard and fast, while nurturing a genius with a camera.

"That's my pre-Kaycee work," he said as he reentered the room.

"You don't do these kinds of pictures anymore?"

He shook his head and placed Kaycee in a playpen in the corner of the room. "Not anymore. The studio now keeps me fairly busy." He looked back at the action photos and Caralie thought she saw a wistfulness in his gaze. She decided it was time to get to the second reason why she was here.

"I want custody of Kaycee." The words blurted out of her.

Riley's eyes widened with shock, then narrowed with animosity. ''Too bad.''

Caralie flushed, realizing she'd handled the initial foray into the subject badly. ''Loretta wanted me to raise the baby—if anything happened to her. I have letters from her stating that.''

''I don't care if you have a mandate from the President. My daughter stays with me.'' His blue eyes had transformed to chips of ice, emanating frosty hostility.

''You didn't even want a baby,'' Caralie protested.

''That was before. This is now.'' He grabbed her coat from the sofa and thrust it toward her, a muscle in his jaw ticking with tension. He looked over at Kaycee, then back at Caralie. ''You come in here spouting crazy stories of murder and now tell me you want custody of my daughter? I think you'd better get a grip on reality.'' His voice was low, as if he didn't want the little girl to hear his words.

''They aren't crazy stories. Somebody killed my sister and I intend to find out who and why.'' Caralie jerked her coat on, desperately trying to control the hot tears that burned at her eyes. ''I've heard the stories about you...Wild Man Riley. Kaycee is a little girl and she needs a woman in her life, not a man with your reputation.''

''Kaycee is my daughter and all she needs is me.'' He opened the door that led to the stairs. ''Now get out.''

Caralie started out the door, then turned back to him, tears beginning to make her vision swim. ''I'll be at the Lone Star Motel if you want to discuss anything further.''

''Our discussion is finished.''

She wanted to make him understand how important it was that she raise Kaycee; needed to make him see that it would be best for the child. She wanted to give to Kaycee all the things she and Loretta had never had—the stability of two parents, the sense of safety and love.

But she knew by the thundercloud of emotions that darkened Riley's features that she'd blown it—approached him all wrong—and that no further rational discussion was possible at this moment.

She stomped down the stairs, angry with him, but more angry with herself. Outside, the unusually cold December air whipped around her, chilling her to the bone as she made her way to where she'd parked her rental car. Tears raced down her cheeks—the first real tears she'd shed since discovering her sister was dead.

She hadn't been here when Loretta had needed her the most, and she hadn't been here in the first months of Kaycee's life. But she was here now, and she intended to solve the mystery of Loretta's murder and spend the rest of her life loving and caring for Kaycee. She certainly wasn't about to let one handsome, sexy Wild Man Riley stand in her way.

Chapter Two

Riley got out of bed just before dawn after a sleepless night. He'd tossed and turned, haunted by visions of Loretta, of Caralie, and finally of his daughter.

As he'd lain on his back in the darkened room, staring blindly up at the ceiling, he'd replayed the phone call from Loretta that had forever changed him. Had she truly been afraid for her life? Had she somehow gotten into life-threatening trouble and made that phone call to him in a last attempt to save herself?

Now he stood at the kitchen counter, groggily waiting for the coffee to finish dripping into the glass carafe. The same thoughts that had haunted the night hours remained with him despite the breaking of dawn. Had the fire at the small hospital in Galveston been set intentionally to kill Loretta? While this particular worry haunted him, another one absolutely terrified him: Could Caralie somehow manage to gain custody of Kaycee?

Riley poured himself a cup of coffee, then sank down at the kitchen table. If he was lucky, he'd manage to drink one cup before his little bundle of dynamite squealed her awakening and demanded his total attention.

By nine o'clock, Riley had not only fed, bathed and dressed Kaycee, but he'd also wrestled with some major decisions. He carried Kaycee out to the car, strapped her into her car seat and headed for the Lone Star Motel.

He would help Caralie explore the circumstances surrounding her sister's death, and not because he owed anything to Caralie, but because he owed it to Kaycee. Besides, surely there was some way he could convince Caralie not to pursue a custody battle.

Kaycee belonged with him, and he'd fight the devil to keep her with him—even if the devil was a woman who had gorgeous gray eyes and long lashes.

The Lone Star Motel was located minutes from Riley's place on the south side of Houston's downtown area. Thankfully when he pulled into the parking lot of the motel there were only three cars parked there. Two of them bore out-of-state plates, and the third one had tags that identified it as a rental car. He guessed that car belonged to Caralie and was parked in front of the unit where she was staying.

For a long moment he remained in the car, wondering if he had made the right decision in coming here. Did he really want to agree to delve into Loretta's life? A woman he'd known intimately, yet hadn't really known at all?

Shame coursed through him as he thought of those distant days of hard work, and harder play, of the kind of man he'd once been. But he was a different kind of man now. Kaycee had given him a reason to change.

The child babbled happily as he got her out of the car seat and carried her to the door of unit 105. He had to make Caralie understand that Wild Man Riley had been tamed and Kaycee belonged with him. Drawing a deep breath, he knocked on the motel-room door.

It was obvious when Caralie opened the door that she'd had a rough night, too. But, she wore her rough night much better than he did. The short white terry-cloth robe she wore emphasized her slender waist and displayed a sinful length of long, tanned legs. Her hair was a tumble of disarray that beckoned his fingers to touch it. She stared at him in surprise, her eyes slightly swollen and red-rimmed.

''We need to talk,'' Riley said.

She frowned and cleared her throat. ''I'll meet you in fifteen minutes in the coffee shop.''

''Okay,'' he replied, unsurprised that she didn't offer to invite him in. He was, after all, a virtual stranger to her, despite the fact that he was the father of her niece.

As she disappeared back into her room, Riley walked across the asphalt parking lot toward the building that identified itself as the motel office and coffee shop. Everywhere were signs of the Christmas season—his first Christmas as a father. Was it possible it might be his last?

It took only moments to get settled in a booth, with Kaycee in a high chair next to him. He ordered a cup of coffee for himself and Caralie and a piece of toast for Kaycee, then settled back to wait for Caralie to arrive.

He'd finished one cup of coffee and had just received a refill when he saw her walking across the pavement. Knowing she was unaware of his scrutiny, he studied her as she approached.

She walked with long, purposeful strides, a pair of jeans hugging her slender legs. A bulky denim jacket hid her shape, but he remembered from the day before when she'd removed her coat, that although slim, she had curves in all the right places. Not that he cared. At the moment she was less an attractive woman and more the enemy who threatened what he loved most.

He smiled at his daughter, who grinned back at him around a soggy section of toast. He thought about wiping her mouth before Caralie got inside, then perversely changed his mind. Let Caralie see how sloppy a child could be and maybe she'd decide motherhood definitely wasn't for her.

He looked up as Caralie appeared at the booth, bringing with her the scent of soap and shampoo and the evocative perfume he'd noticed the day before. Her hair was still damp, and he assumed she'd showered and dressed hurriedly, without taking the time to completely blow her thick hair dry.

She shrugged off her jacket, exposing a navy blue blouse that deepened the gray of her eyes. She slid into the seat opposite him and looked at him expectantly.

"I ordered you coffee," he said, pointing to the cup before her.

"Thanks." She pulled it closer. "I don't normally sleep so late."

"Rough night?" he asked. She nodded and he forced a smile. "For me, too. That's why I'm here." He took a sip of his coffee, then continued. "I spent the entire night thinking about everything you said about Loretta. I'm not sure I believe that somebody intentionally set the fire at the hospital to hurt her, but I'm willing to help you find out what we can about exactly what happened."

She closed her eyes for a moment. When she looked at him again, her eyes radiated gratitude. "Thank you."

"Don't thank me. I'm not doing it for you. I'm doing it for Kaycee. Someday she'll want to know everything about her mother, and I want to be able to answer all her questions."

"It doesn't matter why you've decided to help me. I'm just grateful for the help."

"It doesn't come without a price," Riley said, watching as her eyes narrowed suspiciously.

"What kind of a price?"

"You agree that you won't fight me for custody of Kaycee."

Her cheeks flamed pink. "Sorry, I can't agree to that." She grabbed her purse from the table and stood. "I'll investigate Loretta's death myself."

Riley reached across the table and grabbed her wrist to stop her flight. "Wait. Please, sit down." He released her wrist. Kaycee emitted a wail, apparently sensing the tension in the air between the two adults.

Caralie hesitated, then sank back into the seat. Riley handed Kaycee another piece of toast, smiled reassuringly at the little girl, then looked back at Caralie. "You don't know me at all. It's not fair of you to make a judgment call on my parenting skills based on a reputation I've put behind me."

"All I want is what is in Kaycee's best interests, and I believe she'd be better off with me," Caralie replied.

"She's a lot of trouble. Look at her—she smears her food, and when she's tired she gets really cranky. There are nights she refuses to go to sleep, and she's beginning to develop one heck of a temper."

Caralie smiled, obviously seeing through his ruse. "If she's so terrible, then why would you want to retain custody?"

"Because I love her more than anything or anyone on this earth." Riley's voice shook with naked emotion and Caralie's smile faltered, her eyes changing to the color of turbulent skies.

"And I want to love her," she said softly. "I know what Loretta would have wanted for her." She looked at Kaycee and for the first time Riley saw a wealth of feeling in Caralie's eyes. "Loretta would have wanted her raised with the love of two parents—something she and I never had. I'm...I'm planning on marrying in the next couple of months and providing a stable, loving, two-parent home for Kaycee."

Riley sat back against the booth, his heart thundering with dread. He'd like to think that the fact that he was Kaycee's biological parent would override any threat Caralie might be to his custody, but he knew better.

He was a single man raising a little girl, a man who'd had no real relationship with Kaycee's mother. And there were half-a-dozen old newspaper and magazine articles depicting his former life-style that could be used against him with a conservative judge. Somehow, someway, he had to make Caralie change her mind. He had to make her see how wrong it would be to take Kaycee away from him.

"Look, I can understand your concern. But you don't really know me at all." He leaned forward, an idea taking shape in his mind. "I've got a spare room at my place. Why don't you stay with me until we sort through whatever happened to Loretta. It will give us some time to get to know each other. Judge me by who I am now—not by what I was a year ago. Give me a chance to show you that Kaycee is where she belongs."

"I don't know if that's a good idea...." she began hesitantly.

"Why not? It will give you an opportunity not only to get to know me better, but to get to know Kaycee." He paused, his heart in his throat as he contemplated his next words.

"I couldn't stand the thought of Kaycee being wrenched away from me and into the arms of a virtual stranger. This might help Kaycee adjust to any changes that might take place in the future." He coughed to rid his voice of emotion. "Besides, I've got Loretta's things from her apartment packed in boxes in my basement. We can go through them and see if there're any clues as to what was going on in Loretta's life before the fire."

"How did you get Loretta's belongings?"

"I didn't know she had any relatives and when she died I contacted her landlady at the apartment where she'd been living and she boxed up the personal items for me." He shrugged and took a sip of his coffee. "I didn't know what else to do. I thought eventually I'd want Loretta's things for Kaycee."

"Have you been through them at all?" she asked.

He shook his head. "When I first picked them up, I had a newborn baby to adjust to and simply didn't take the time to go through the boxes and see exactly what was there. I still haven't taken the time." He shoved his empty coffee cup aside. "So, what do you say? Can we make a deal of some kind? You come and stay with me and hold off making any kind of a move for custody. In return, I'll do whatever I can to help you investigate the circumstances of Loretta's death."

She stared at him thoughtfully, obviously trying to decide what to do. Riley remained silent, giving her time to think through all her options. He wasn't sure that a few days was enough time for him to convince her to leave Kaycee where she was, but at least it bought him a couple of days to think about how to fight her.

He relaxed somewhat when he saw her answer in her eyes. "Okay," she agreed.

THERE WAS NO WAY Caralie intended to forget the issue of custody. She wanted Kaycee. She needed

Kaycee. But she also wanted to find out what had happened to her sister; and if Loretta had been murdered, Caralie wouldn't rest until justice was done.

Although she knew she could get to the bottom of Loretta's death on her own, it would take her longer than if she had Riley's help. She'd only been in Houston once before and didn't know the city. Besides, she hoped Loretta's personal effects would yield a clue, and at the moment Riley was the keeper of those effects.

It took them only a few minutes to gather Caralie's belongings together and check her out of the motel. As she followed Riley back to his house, she wondered if agreeing to stay with him was a mistake.

Something about him drew her—the dark mystery in his eyes, the appeal of his handsome features. She knew he'd had a reputation as a womanizer, had rarely been seen twice with the same beautiful woman on his arm. The one thing she couldn't afford to do was be seduced by his attractiveness. She had to remember he was everything she didn't like in a man, despite the fact that he made her pulse race just a tad bit faster.

However, despite her reticence about staying with him, she wasn't exactly wealthy, had only a small savings account and had worried about how many days and nights at the motel she could charge to her credit card without it exploding.

She'd had to pay an obscene amount of money to get her plane ticket. That it was the holiday season, coupled with the fact that she hadn't made advance plans, had gouged her with a price that rivaled the national debt.

At least staying with Riley alleviated the need for a motel room. She followed his car to the back of his studio and parked beside him.

"Here, let me help you with those," he said as she pulled two suitcases out of her trunk. With Kaycee in one arm, he grabbed one of the suitcases and Caralie followed behind with the other. "We'll get you squared away in the spare room, then start sorting through Loretta's things to see what we can find."

Caralie nodded, her heart quickening with thoughts of Loretta. She still couldn't believe her sister was gone; had yet to allow her abiding grief to surface. She would eventually grieve long and hard, but first she wanted to find out exactly what had happened. It wasn't enough just to know that Loretta had died in a fire.

"It's small, but functional," Riley said as he opened the door to the bedroom where she would be staying.

The room contained only a single bed, a dresser and a wall of built-in shelves. The spread was navy blue, still retaining the creases that pronounced it brand-new.

"The bathroom is right across the hall and there should be empty hangers in the closet. Feel free to use the drawers in the dresser. They're all empty right now," Riley said.

"Thanks," Caralie replied as she placed her suitcase on the bed.

"I'll just let you get unpacked." Riley disappeared farther down the hallway, leaving her alone in the room—alone with her thoughts.

It took her only minutes to unpack and hang what few clothes she had. Her work experience in Africa had taught her to travel light.

It sometimes frightened her how little she had to show for her twenty-five years on earth. When she'd decided to take the job and travel to Africa, she'd given most of her furniture and clothing to Loretta. At that time, Caralie and Loretta had been living in St. Louis. Caralie could only assume that when Loretta had decided to move to Houston, she'd either sold or left behind Caralie's things.

After unpacking, she shoved the empty suitcases into the bottom of the closet, then left the bedroom and wandered back into the living room.

Riley was nowhere around, but Kaycee sat in her playpen, cooing and babbling as she played with a set of foam blocks. She looked up and cast Caralie a bewitching smile as Caralie drew closer.

Caralie sat on a chair near the playpen, drinking in the sight of the child who possessed so many of her mother's physical characteristics in miniature. Kaycee pulled herself up to a wobbly standing position and held out one of the blocks toward Caralie.

As Caralie started to take it, Kaycee threw it, then laughed in delight. "You little minx." Caralie smiled as she retrieved the block and handed it back to Kaycee. She threw it again, apparently enthralled by the game of fetch.

"Ah, I see she's trapped you into participating in

her favorite game,'' Riley observed as he entered the living room. Caralie laughed as Kaycee pitched the block yet again. ''And I promise, you'll tire of it, long before she does.''

She chased after the block several more times, intensely aware of Riley's gaze focused on her, an amused smile curving his sensual mouth. ''Okay, I surrender,'' she exclaimed as she flopped into the chair to catch her breath.

Riley laughed, a deep rumbly baritone of pleasure that sent an echoing warmth coursing through her. He scooped Kaycee up in his arms. ''We'll give this kid some lunch, then put her down for a nap. While she's napping we'll go downstairs and start sorting through the boxes.''

Caralie followed the two into the kitchen. As Riley settled Kaycee in her high chair, Caralie sat down at the table, her gaze still focused on the little girl.

''You hungry?'' Riley asked her.

Caralie shook her head. ''Not really.''

''Okay, I'll feed Kaycee for now and we can grab something later.'' Within minutes, he placed Kaycee's plate before her on the high-chair tray, then sat down across from Caralie.

''She looks so much like Loretta,'' Caralie observed as she watched Kaycee eat.

''She looks a lot like you.''

''People sometimes mistook Loretta and me for twins, despite our age difference.''

''Are you the younger sister or the older one?'' Riley asked.

"Younger by two years." She frowned, remembering their growing-up years. "And older in most other ways. Loretta was a wonderful, warm woman, but she was also irresponsible and often made horrible choices without thinking through the consequences."

She swallowed around a lump of grief. "That's why I'm so afraid she got into trouble—got into something way over her head." She looked at him curiously. "Where did you meet her?"

"In a club. I'd just gotten back to the States and several friends took me out to a new dance club to welcome me back and celebrate my twenty-eighth birthday." His face flushed slightly. "I have to admit, it was a crazy night. I'd just returned from Mexico, where I'd taken pictures of a devastating earthquake." He leaned back in his chair and swiped a hand through his dark hair, his features reflecting the destruction he'd witnessed. "I had the smell of death in my nose, tasted it in my mouth, and that night all I wanted was to feel alive."

"And so you slept with Loretta?" Despite Caralie's desire to keep the question devoid of emotion, she heard the condemnation in her tone.

"Ah, there you go, believing my press," he returned with a touch of coolness. "No, I didn't sleep with her that night. We danced together, and we talked." He smiled, as if remembering that night. "Your sister made me laugh. She was so filled with life, seemed so eager to embrace it. We saw each other every night for a week and one thing led to another and we fell into a physical relationship.''

''What happened? Why did you stop seeing each other?''

Riley shrugged. ''I'm not really sure. I had to go to California for a shoot and when I got back into town, her number had been changed and I never heard from her again until the night before the fire.''

They both jumped as Kaycee banged on her now empty plate. The baby laughed, delighted to have their undivided attention. ''Come on, you little stinker, let's get you cleaned up and ready for a nap,'' Riley exclaimed. He washed her face and hands, then lifted her from the high chair.

''Riley, would you mind... I mean, could I put her down for her nap?'' Caralie stood hesitantly, watching the emotions that played across his face at her request.

''Okay...sure.'' He moved closer so Caralie could take the little girl from his arms.

Kaycee came willingly to Caralie. ''Are there any nap-time rituals I need to follow?'' she asked.

''She likes to cuddle the gray stuffed kitty and she likes her back rubbed,'' Riley replied. He turned away from them and busied himself cleaning off the high chair.

Caralie carried Kaycee down the hallway. As Kaycee laid her head against Caralie's shoulder, Caralie breathed in the sweet scent of the little girl, for the first time allowing her emotions loose where Kaycee was concerned.

''Sweet baby,'' Caralie murmured. Kaycee nuzzled closer, and placed her hand on Caralie's cheek. Tears burned hot in Caralie's eyes. Her niece. The only family she had left in the entire world.

The nursery was a small but pleasant room, complete with crib, change table, and wallpaper borders of smiling stars and benevolent moon faces.

Caralie placed Kaycee in the crib, then grabbed the scruffy but obviously well-loved gray kitty from the top of the dresser. The little girl hugged the stuffed animal, then flopped down on her stomach as if awaiting Caralie's caress on her back.

Caralie felt her defenses breaking down, allowing into her heart the enormous love for—the incredible wonder of—her sister's child. She stroked Kaycee's back until the baby's eyes drifted closed and her breathing deepened to the rhythm of sleep. Still, Caralie remained leaning over the edge of the crib, reluctant to break the tenuous connection between herself and her niece.

It had been so long since she'd allowed herself to feel, permitted herself the luxury of dropping the protective shell she'd wrapped around her heart.

''I was beginning to wonder if maybe she'd put you to sleep.''

Caralie looked up to see Riley standing in the doorway, his expression enigmatic. Caralie gave Kaycee a final rub on her back, then reluctantly joined Riley at the door. ''She's such a sweetheart,'' Caralie said as they walked back down the hallway toward the kitchen.

"I didn't think you thought so yesterday."

She looked at him in surprise. "What do you mean?"

"I don't know.... You seemed sort of stiff with her, like you were afraid she might mess up your hair or get your face sticky."

Caralie smiled with a touch of sadness. "One of the first things I learned when I started working with the children in those African villages was to maintain an emotional distance. So many of them were deathly sick and undernourished, objectivity became a survival instinct for me."

Riley nodded. "Like me taking pictures of disasters. I had to keep myself separate from what I was seeing."

"Exactly," Caralie exclaimed, pleased with his understanding. "Yesterday, I wasn't sure I wasn't going to have to fight you to be a part of Kaycee's life, so I was afraid to allow myself to feel too much for her." She smiled. "But it's impossible to hold back love where she's concerned, isn't it?"

Riley's eyes were cool, distant. "We'd better get downstairs and start going through those boxes while she's napping."

Caralie followed him down a set of stairs that led past the studio on the first floor and into the basement below. She had to remember that despite the fact that Riley had been Loretta's lover and was Kaycee's father, in spite of the fact he'd agreed to help her find out exactly what had happened to Loretta, he wasn't Caralie's friend.

She and Riley would eventually meet in a court of law to battle for custody of Kaycee. Just as she knew she'd use whatever ammunition she could against him, she knew he'd do the same.

No, he wasn't her friend. At the moment they were uneasy comrades beginning an investigation into Loretta's death. Nothing more.

The basement was small but neat, with various-sized boxes packed against one wall. There were approximately fifteen boxes marked with Loretta's name in bold black marker on the sides.

"This is everything?" Caralie asked.

Riley nodded. "At the time of the fire she was living in an exclusive apartment with good furniture, but according to the landlady it was all rented."

Caralie frowned, wondering how her sister had paid rent on such an exclusive apartment. "Do you know what Loretta was doing for work?"

"No. At the time I was seeing her, I just assumed she had enough money so that work wasn't necessary, but we didn't talk about it." He pulled a large box from the top of the pile and set in on the floor in front of Caralie. "As we finish with each box I'll stack them over there." He pointed to the opposite side of the room. "That way we won't get mixed up and double the work."

The first couple of boxes yielded nothing but clothing...clothing far more expensive than Caralie had ever known Loretta to own.

As they worked, side by side, exploring Loretta's life through the items she'd left behind, Caralie tried to ignore the clean, masculine scent that emanated from Riley. She tried to avoid noticing the way his biceps bulged against the fabric of his shirt each time he lifted a box, how his jeans clung to his long legs as if fitted specifically to him.

Caralie couldn't remember the last time she'd been physically attracted to a man. Certainly, she didn't feel that way about David.

David Westfall was the man she'd probably marry—a man she admired and had worked with for the past two years. Although David didn't make her heart beat faster, didn't stir the same kind of unsettling emotions that Riley stirred in her, David felt safe. Whatever it was that Riley awakened within her felt distinctly unsafe.

"Bingo!" he cried, tugging her from her thoughts. "This looks like a box of paperwork."

Caralie moved over to the box and together she and Riley began sorting through the jumble of sales receipts, scraps of paper and bundles of old letters. They started a pile of the papers that held names and phone numbers, knowing their next course of action would be to contact those people and see what their relationship was to Loretta.

They were halfway through the box when Riley pulled out a sheet of paper and cursed softly beneath his breath. "What?" Caralie asked, the expression on his face causing her heart to thud anxiously.

Without saying a word, he handed her the piece of paper. Caralie stared down at it, her hand trembling slightly. Written in red marker, in bold, block letters, were the words:

TALK TO ANYONE AND YOU DIE.

Caralie's blood chilled as she stared at the warning that confirmed what she'd felt all along. Loretta had been in trouble. Somebody had killed her. And Caralie wouldn't rest until she knew who—and why.

Chapter Three

''Oh, Riley.'' Caralie looked at him, knowing her fear was in her eyes for him to see. ''Loretta *was* in trouble.''

''It certainly looks that way.'' He frowned and dug through the remaining papers in the box, then pulled out another note written in red marker.

DEAD WOMEN TELL NO TALES.

A muscle ticked in his jaw. ''Dammit, I should have asked her more questions that night when she called me. I should have insisted she meet me immediately.''

Caralie placed a hand on his shoulder, knowing that despite the fact that logic dictated that neither one of them should feel guilty, he obviously felt as culpable as she.

If only she hadn't left the States; if only she hadn't decided to force Loretta to fend for herself. ''I don't understand this. Why didn't the police find these notes in Loretta's apartment? Why didn't they check into her past? Why didn't they launch an investigation into her death?'' She dropped her hand from his shoulder as he stood and grabbed the box from the floor.

''I don't know. Let's talk upstairs. I need to check on Kaycee and we can finish going through this box up there.''

Caralie nodded and pulled herself up off the floor. She felt soul-weary, floundering in a sea of too many questions and too few answers. The ache of Loretta's absence resounded deep inside her, making her feel a yawning disconnection from everyone else in the world.

She followed Riley up the stairs and into the kitchen. He placed the box on the table, then excused himself to go check on Kaycee. When Riley left the room, Caralie sank into a chair at the table and stared at the box, her heart aching with a heavy burden of grief.

As children, she and Loretta had promised to always stay together, and despite the fact that Caralie had been the younger of the two, it had been she who had promised to always take care of her sister—a promise she had broken. And now, Loretta was gone.

However, fate hadn't left her with nothing. There was Loretta's child—a little angel named Kaycee—and Caralie was determined that she would do for Kaycee what she hadn't been able to do for Loretta.

She looked up as Riley came back into the room. ''She's still sleeping,'' he said. ''How about I make us some sandwiches and we can eat while we talk?''

Caralie nodded, realizing she was starving. She hadn't eaten anything since noon the day before. "What can I do to help?"

"Nothing, I can handle a couple of sandwiches. Ham and cheese all right?" He moved the box from the table to the floor nearby.

"Fine."

As Riley set to work, pulling items from the refrigerator and placing them on the counter, Caralie found herself studying him. He moved with a graceful economy, looking completely at home in the kitchen; and yet it was easy to imagine him in a dangerous setting, shooting photos to inform and educate the world.

She stirred, uncomfortable with the crazy, unwanted attraction she felt for him. "So, tell me about the investigation into the fire."

"I don't know too much about it. For a couple of days immediately after the fire, there were articles in the newspaper, some follow-up on the evening news." He put their plates on the table, each one laden with a sandwich and potato chips. "Soda?" She nodded and he went back to the refrigerator and grabbed two cans.

"You have to remember," he said as he rejoined her at the table, "at the time the investigation was going on, I'd just found myself the single parent of a newborn baby. I not only had to buy all the things required to take care of Kaycee, I also had to readjust my work schedule to accommodate my newfound fatherhood."

Eventually, Riley will come to thank me for taking

custody of Kaycee, Caralie told herself. He'd be able to go back to the kind of life he'd been leading before Kaycee's birth. Travel and excitement, partying until dawn, enjoying the company of beautiful women—surely he missed all that.

Caralie nibbled on a potato chip thoughtfully. ''Didn't the police investigate Loretta at all? Didn't they check into her past? Find out if she had any enemies?''

''Loretta's death wasn't the focus of the investigation,'' he explained.

''I don't understand. How could that be? Were there other deaths?''

Riley paused for a moment and took a bite of his sandwich, following it with a drink of soda. ''No, Loretta was the only fatality, but her room was closest to the storage area where the fire was started. The authorities believed her death was simply a matter of her being in the wrong place at the wrong time. Besides, the night of the fire, from what I remember, three babies were born and in the chaos of the aftermath, they discovered one of those babies had been kidnapped.''

''Oh, how terrible,'' Caralie gasped, unable to imagine the depth of the horror of giving birth and then learning the child was gone—stolen. ''Did they find the baby? Did the kidnapping have something to do with the fire?''

Somehow, Caralie knew it would give her a modicum of peace to discover that Loretta's death had, indeed, simply been a tragic mistake rather than a calculated murder.

Riley frowned, the gesture creating a wrinkle across his forehead and deepening the lines on either side of his mouth. "If I remember right, the mother and baby were reunited and it was discovered that the fire had nothing to do with the kidnapping."

"Then we're back to the possibility that the fire was set specifically to harm Loretta." Caralie picked up her sandwich and took a bite, chewing self-consciously as she felt Riley's eyes on her.

She looked up to find him studying her, the intensity of his gaze pulling a blush to her cheeks. "I understand why it's so important to know, but you realize it's possible you might never learn the answers. I mean, it's been eight months. Even if Loretta was murdered, it doesn't change the circumstances we're all in right now. She's gone, and nothing we find out now is going to bring her back."

His tone was gentle, but Caralie winced beneath the harsh reality the words contained. "I know nothing will bring Loretta back." She looked down at her plate, trying to think how to explain to him why she had to know exactly what had happened to her sister. She glanced up again. "Did you grow up in a family, Riley? Were you raised by a mother and father?"

His dark brows danced upward quizzically. "Sure, although my dad passed away a couple of years ago."

Caralie set her sandwich back on her plate. "Loretta and I were raised in a series of foster homes." She mentally detoured around some of the more painful memories of those years. "I was six and Loretta was eight when our mother dropped us off at a local shelter and never returned. We quickly learned to depend solely on each other.''

She sighed impatiently, realizing it was impossible to make him understand. Besides, she didn't want to bare her heart to this man who might take any information she gave him and use it against her when she made a bid for custody of Kaycee. ''We promised we'd always take care of each other, that we'd always be there for one another.''

She sighed again. ''I can't just let this go. If Loretta was murdered, then the guilty person must be punished.... And I need to know why she was killed,'' she added softly.

''Then it looks like we're going to launch a murder investigation,'' he replied.

Caralie smiled at him gratefully. For just a moment she wanted to lean into him, feel his arms around her in silent support. She wanted to be held against his firm, strong chest, feel connected with him as they began their quest.

Instead, she once again picked up her sandwich. It would be crazy for her to get emotionally involved on any level with Riley. It would only make it more difficult for both of them when she eventually faced him in a court of law. ''So, where do we begin our investigation?''

''I suppose the logical place to begin is the hospital.''

''The one in Galveston?'' she asked.

He shook his head. ''The Galveston hospital is still being rebuilt. All the staff and patients were moved to the Houston hospital immediately after the fire.''

''Why would Loretta go to a hospital in Galveston instead of one right here in Houston?'' she wondered aloud.

''When I went to pick up Kaycee, I asked the nurse if she knew why Loretta had chosen to have her baby at the Galveston facility instead of one here in town. She told me Loretta's doctor, Gregory Barnes, had moved his practice to Galveston about four months before, and Loretta was one of his patients who'd opted to remain under his care despite the distance.''

Caralie nodded. ''That makes sense. I can't imagine a woman wanting to change doctors in the middle of a pregnancy.''

Riley looked at his watch. ''By the time Kaycee gets up from her nap, it will be too late to go to the hospital today. I'll make arrangements with my mother to watch Kaycee tomorrow and we'll go from there.''

Caralie reached across the table and touched his hand lightly. ''Thank you, Riley. This is important to me and I appreciate your help.''

He withdrew his hand from her touch, his dark eyes not unfriendly, but offering little warmth. ''I told you before, I'm not doing this for you. I'm doing it for Kaycee. She's the only thing that matters to me.''

Caralie met his challenging stare with one of her own, thankful that with his words he'd reminded her that they were not partners, but rather, opponents in a struggle for Loretta's child—a struggle Caralie intended to win.

RILEY OPENED HIS EYES and looked at the glowing dial of the clock next to his bed. One in the morning. Something had awakened him, but he wasn't sure what.

He remained unmoving, listening to hear if perhaps Kaycee had cried out. It was rare for her to wake up in the night, but occasionally she did. A kiss and a rub on the back usually put her to sleep again.

Maybe it hadn't been any noise at all that had awakened him. Maybe it had simply been the cacophony of his internal thoughts and worries.

Not only was he worried about keeping custody of Kaycee, but he had to admit, uncovering those notes among Loretta's things had deeply disturbed him. Who had written them? What sort of trouble had Loretta found?

He threw back the covers and sat up, knowing further sleep, at least for now, would be impossible. He started to leave the bedroom clad only in his undershorts, then remembered he had a houseguest. He grabbed his bathrobe from the hook on the back of the bedroom door and pulled the material around him as he left his room.

He paused in the doorway of the living room, realizing what had most likely awakened him. Caralie sat in a chair, staring at the Christmas-tree lights, which he'd forgotten to turn off before going to bed.

She didn't appear to realize he was there and he took the opportunity to watch her, study her. She looked small, achingly vulnerable, wrapped in her terry-cloth robe and curled up in the wing chair.

He remembered what she'd told him, about being raised in a series of foster homes, her sister her only connection. And now that sister was gone, possibly murdered. He recognized that if he dwelled on those thoughts, a tiny wedge of compassion might bloom in his heart, and that was the last thing he wanted. He didn't want to feel sorry for her, didn't want to feel charitable toward a woman who just might very well be successful in taking the only thing that mattered from him.

"Couldn't sleep?"

She started at the sound of his voice and looked at him, her eyes luminous. "No." She smiled wryly. "Guess it's something of an epidemic."

"Yeah." He sat in the chair across from her, noting how the reflected Christmas-tree lights danced on the dark cloud of her hair.

"I know it sounds crazy, but I'd forgotten it was Christmas until I tried to get a ticket back home." She played with her belt ends, lacing and unlacing them as she spoke. "Loretta and I never made much of the traditional holidays." A ghost of a smile curved her lips. "We made up our own special days to celebrate."

"Like Official Popcorn Day?"

Her eyes widened in surprise. "She told you about that?"

"She didn't exactly tell me. I was with her on the day she said was Official Popcorn Day and we spent that afternoon going from one store to another buying bags of different flavors of popcorn."

Caralie laughed, the pleasant sound shooting a coil

of heat through Riley. "Oh, gosh, I'd forgotten all about it. July 28th, right?"

He nodded. "That sounds about right. It was just before I left on assignment."

She smiled and looked back at the tree. "We made a pact. I must have been about ten and Loretta twelve. We decided that popcorn needed its own special day and on that day when we got older, we'd eat all the popcorn we could." She laughed again. "Silly, isn't it."

She straightened in the chair, sliding her feet down primly to the floor, obviously unaware that it merely served to give him a better view of her shapely legs. "Did you have a good Christmas?"

"Yeah, it was nice. My mom came over and spent the day here. She adores Kaycee." Riley added the last words purposely, to inform her that Kaycee had a grandmother who loved her. Caralie wouldn't just be taking the little girl away from him, but away from his mother, as well.

"You're close to your mother?"

There was a slight wistfulness in her voice that again stirred a flurry of compassion in Riley. He consciously tamped it down. "We're closer now than we've ever been. When I was traveling so much, it was difficult to maintain any sort of personal relationships." He looked at her curiously. "Didn't you find the same thing true in your travels in Africa? This man you intend to marry—your fiancé—is he here in the States?"

"No, we work together." She shifted positions once again, averting her gaze from his. "And he isn't officially my fiancé. I mean, he's asked me to marry him, but I haven't accepted his proposal yet. But, I'm going to.'' She raised her chin defiantly. ''I'm sure we'll be married and settled in the next month or so.''

She didn't sound like a woman in love, nor did her eyes have the starry-eyed gleam of a woman eager to rush into the vows of matrimony. Rather she sounded like a woman willing to do whatever was necessary to reach her goal—and her goal was to take his daughter away from him.

''I hope the two of you will be very happy and have lots of children of your own,'' he said pointedly, knowing on some subconscious level it was an effort to pick a fight.

Her eyes widened and her mouth opened. Instantly he steeled himself for the heated retort he expected to follow. Instead she narrowed her eyes, swallowed visibly, then smiled. ''It's only two days after Christmas, Riley. Maybe we should practice a little 'peace on earth.' We won't settle the issue of Kaycee's custody by sniping at each other.''

''You're right,'' he agreed, irritated with himself. He'd invited her into his home to prove to her what a great guy he was and already he was blowing it.

''So, tell me about Kaycee's first Christmas. What did Santa Claus bring her?'' Caralie leaned forward, her eyes pools of dancing colors as they reflected the lights from the tree.

Riley looked away from her, finding her far too alluring for comfort. As she'd leaned forward he'd caught a glimpse of navy silk beneath the white robe;

and beneath the whisper of midnight silk, the creamy curves of her breasts.

"I got her one of those cloth dolls with buttons and snaps and zippers. It's supposed to be educational." His heart swelled as he thought of those moments when he and his mother had helped Kaycee open Santa's surprises. "She got a purple hippo that she can sit on and ride, and a telephone that talks...." He felt the smile in his heart make its way to his lips. "But her favorite of all the things Santa brought was the colorful wrapping paper. She tore it. She wore it. She ate it."

Caralie laughed and again a ripple of warmth swept through him at the melodic sound. And in that sweet warmth, Riley sensed danger.

Claustrophobia set in as he realized the seductive intimacy of the scene. Two people in their nightclothes in the darkness of the night, the only illumination the romantic glow of twinkling Christmas-tree lights.

He stood abruptly, and she started at his sudden movement. "It's late," he said as he strode toward the doorway. "I'm going back to bed." He paused and looked at her. "We've got a full day planned tomorrow. You should try to get some sleep."

She nodded. "I will. I just want to sit here for a little while longer." She looked back at the glowing, decorated pine tree. "The lights are soothing."

Riley gazed at her for another long moment. She was a curious mix of contradictions. Right now, she radiated a compelling vulnerability.

Loretta had possessed the same quality, wearing

her neediness on her shirtsleeve. But with Loretta, it hadn't taken Riley long to discern that there was very little more to Loretta's character than her overwhelming neediness.

Caralie was different. In her, he sensed a core of steel, a center of strength. He had a feeling that despite the aura of vulnerability she radiated, Caralie was strong enough to achieve whatever she set out to do. If she succeeded with her threats to take his child, she'd rip his very heart in two.

Chapter Four

Despite the fact that Caralie had slept little and what little sleep she'd gotten had been plagued by nightmares of smoke and fire, she awoke with the dawn.

Through the window the slowly rising sun splashed color across the sky. Inch by inch the vivid hues shoved away the darkness of night to make way for the new day.

Hopefully, the day she got some answers. She hadn't been able to fully explain to Riley why it was so important she find out exactly what had happened to Loretta. In truth, she wasn't sure herself. She only knew that her life couldn't go forward until she'd learned the real reasons for Loretta's death.

She crept from her bed and into the bathroom across the hall, the utter silence of the house telling her that Kaycee and Riley still slept.

As she stood beneath the hot spray of the shower, she tried to summon David's features into her mind, but the vision kept transforming itself into Riley's face.

Riley, with his dangerously sexy eyes, sensual

mouth and the dancing dimple in one cheek that appeared when he smiled. Riley, who somehow managed to make her feel on edge, like an electric current had run amok inside her whenever he looked at her. Riley, who—according to Loretta's letters—had made it clear he wanted no children, no wife, no emotional entanglements to stifle his freewheeling lifestyle.

At the moment, he was probably intrigued by the novelty of being a father. Eventually he'd be relieved to be rid of the lifelong responsibility of raising a child.

By the time Caralie had dressed, braided her damp hair and left the bathroom, the scent of freshly-brewed coffee beckoned from the kitchen.

"Good morning," Riley greeted her as she entered. He sat at the table, a cup of coffee before him. It was obvious he'd just showered, as well. His thick dark hair was still wet and the scent of minty soap and shaving cream battled with the fragrance of the coffee. "Help yourself." He gestured to the pot.

"Thanks." She poured herself a cup, then joined him at the table. "I've been thinking about all the items we found in that box of personal papers of Loretta's," she said.

"And?"

"And it suddenly struck me that more telling than what we found is what we didn't find."

He frowned. "I don't understand."

"Besides those threatening notes, we found names and phone numbers scribbled on scrap paper, canceled checks from two years ago, an insurance policy on a car she no longer owns. There were even bumper stickers and political buttons for some guy running for mayor. But what we didn't find were stubs from paychecks, receipts for rent payment and utility bills. Where was Loretta working? How was she living?''

''Maybe we'll find some of those answers today. Somebody has to know something about Loretta's personal life for the past year or so.''

Caralie took a sip of her coffee. ''I know when I left for Africa, she was working as a bartender in a place called Tommy's Tavern.''

''Here in Houston?'' Riley asked. Caralie nodded and Riley stood and went to one of the cabinets. He pulled out a phone book and thumbed through the pages.

Caralie took another drink of her coffee, watching him. Clad in a long-sleeved black turtleneck and worn black jeans, he looked handsome and thoroughly male. The clingy cotton shirt emphasized his broad back and bulging biceps, and the jeans hugged his slender hips and long legs.

Again Caralie attempted to summon a mental image of David—but couldn't. It was as if Riley's physical presence made thinking of another man utterly impossible.

''Ah, here we go. Tommy's Tavern. It's on the south side of town in a rather seedy area.'' He closed the phone book and turned back to Caralie. ''If you think it would help at all, we can swing by. Maybe somebody knows where Loretta went to work after she left there.''

Caralie stared at Riley intently. "When you were seeing Loretta, she didn't mention any work? She didn't talk about people she was involved with? Personal things about her everyday life?"

He sank back in his chair at the table and swiped a hand through his hair in obvious frustration. "It was a deal we made when we first met. We agreed not to talk about our pasts or our futures. I know it sounds crazy, but for the two weeks that I dated her, we just lived from moment to moment. We went to the movies, we ate out. We filled every minute of every day with fun. The one thing we didn't do was really talk."

He sighed, the sound holding a whisper of guilt. "I thought we'd have time later. I figured when I got back from assignment we'd have time to get to know each other on a more cerebral level."

Caralie stared into her cup, somehow unsurprised by his words. Loretta had never liked to talk, had always had a frenzied need to stay out of her own head, away from her own thoughts. "She lived each day in the present because the past was too painful and the future too filled with uncertainty." She looked up to meet Riley's gaze.

"What about you? You had the same experiences as Loretta, right? Do you live only in the present?" he asked.

She shook her head. "I've always looked ahead, planned my future and worked hard to achieve my goals. Loretta was weak. She needed people in her life to make her feel good about herself. I don't need anyone in my life but me. I choose the people I let in through want, not need.''

''Sounds lonely,'' he observed softly.

''It's not,'' she countered. ''It's...just the way I am.'' She took a sip from her cup, surprised to realize she'd almost said that it was ''safe.'' How odd. She dismissed the thought as Kaycee cried from the bedroom.

''Ah, the princess awakens,'' Riley said. He jumped up, as if afraid Caralie might beat him to it. ''I'll go get her and be right back.''

He disappeared down the hallway and a moment later Caralie heard his deep voice and Kaycee's responding babble.

An hour later, Riley was driving them toward his mother's house. Kaycee was buckled into her infant seat in the back, the beloved stuffed kitty in her lap. Caralie sat on the passenger side, watching her niece play with the plush animal.

Traffic was heavy with after-Christmas shoppers seeking bargains. Plastic candy canes hung from traffic lights and street signs, vivid reminders of the season.

It seemed almost macabre that with carols tinkling out of stores and residual Christmas joy on people's faces, she and Riley were on a mission to find a possible murderer.

After ten minutes or so, Riley pulled up in front of an attractive two-story home in a pleasant residential neighborhood. ''I'll just wait here in the car,'' Caralie told him. She didn't want to meet Riley's mother, needed to keep emotional distance from her as well as from Riley if she intended to follow through on her bid for custody of Kaycee.

"Suit yourself," Riley replied. He got out of the car, then leaned into the back to unbuckle Kaycee. Caralie watched as father and daughter disappeared into the house.

She was unsure what to make of Riley Kincaid. So far, she'd seen little justification for his nickname "Wild Man Riley," by the press. But of course, he'd be on his best behavior with her, she reminded herself. Give him time and his true colors would show. A leopard didn't change spots, even when that leopard became a father.

She watched as he bounded out of the house and back to the car, his long legs carrying him with a graceful ease. He slid in behind the steering wheel and flashed her a quick smile. "Okay, we're on our way. First stop...Galveston." He pulled away from the curb.

"Galveston? What's there? I thought you said all the hospital staff had been moved to a hospital here in Houston."

"They have, but I figured the logical place to start is with the arson investigator in charge of the case. It's been months since I've heard anything. It's possible the mystery of the fire has been solved and I didn't hear anything about it."

"How far is it to Galveston?"

"About a fifty-minute drive." He cast her a quick glance. "You've never been there?"

She shook her head. "This is my first trip to Texas."

"And where did you say you were from?"

"St. Louis. Loretta and I had a little apartment together there. When I decided to join David on the mission to Africa, Loretta wanted to make a change, as well. She'd met a couple of people who lived in Houston and decided to move here." She shifted in her seat, turning slightly to look at him. "What about you? Have you always lived in Houston?"

"Always. I was raised in the house where my mom still lives. Although I traveled a lot, I never really considered moving anyplace else. Houston has always felt like home."

A touch of envy swept through Caralie. She'd never had a place that felt like home. Each and every place she'd lived had always felt temporary, as if she were in a holding pattern, waiting for something—but she didn't know what.

Soon, she promised herself. Soon she'd build that place called "home" with David and Kaycee. And "happily ever after" would finally be within her grasp.

RILEY DIVIDED HIS attention between the road in front of him and the woman beside him. Caralie slept, her soft, rhythmic breathing barely audible above the hum of the engine. Her long lashes cast shadows beneath her eyes and her lips were slightly open, as if awaiting a lover's kiss.

He tightened his grip on the steering wheel and focused his concentration out the front windshield. His mother had given him hell for aiding Caralie in her desire to discover exactly what had happened to Loretta.

''Instead of traipsing around the city trying to find out what happened over eight months ago, you should be hiring a lawyer to defend your custody of Kaycee!'' Margaret Riley had exclaimed. Her eyes had blazed with the protectiveness of a mama bear.

Riley knew his mother was probably right. He should be finding a good lawyer and preparing himself for a custody battle. He should be getting a private investigator to delve into Caralie's life and find weaknesses that could be used against her.

Instead, he was driving her to Galveston on what probably would turn out to be a wild-goose chase. Despite the notes they had found among Loretta's personal belongings, Riley had a difficult time believing that somebody had put an entire hospital of patients at risk just to murder Loretta.

So, why was he here instead of in a lawyer's office? Once again, without volition, his gaze took in Caralie. What was it about her that made him want to help her? What quality did she possess that touched him, made him feel uncomfortable and yet unable to deny her his aid?

As he hit the Galveston city limits, she stirred, shrugging off her sleep and straightening in her seat. She frowned, as if disoriented. ''Wha— Where are we?''

''Galveston,'' he answered.

She shot him a self-conscious smile. ''Whew, I can't believe I was so soundly asleep.''

He returned her smile. "You obviously needed it."

"It's been a rough couple of days. But everything will be easier once I have some answers."

"You might not get those answers today," he cautioned. He didn't want her to be overly optimistic about what the day might bring.

"I know. But at least I'll feel like we've started the process of finding out what happened."

Riley turned into the parking area of the Galveston Police Department. The department was housed in a two-story building surrounded by well-kept shrubs and flowers that appeared to thrive in the cool weather.

"Smell the ocean?" he asked as they got out of the car. The air smelled of foaming shoreline—a tang of salt and the slightly unpleasant odor of fish.

She nodded and pulled the collar of her jacket closer around her neck. "It's cooler here." She shivered and Riley guessed it was more likely nerves than the outside temperature that made her shudder.

He felt an impulse to pull her against him, warm her up and give her the courage to face whatever lay ahead. But, before he could follow through on the feeling, she took a deep breath and straightened her shoulders, obviously drawing on her own internal strength.

"We'd like to speak to whoever was in charge of the investigation into the Galveston hospital fire," Riley said to the officer behind the front desk.

"That would be Sergeant Farrell." He pointed to

a bench against the wall. "Have a seat and I'll see if he's available."

Together Riley and Caralie sat on the bench, their thighs brushing as they settled back on the hard wood. Riley tried to focus on the questions he intended to ask the investigator, but found concentration difficult with the scent of Caralie's perfume eddying in the air around him.

Uncomfortable with the stir of emotion it evoked, he leaned forward in an effort to escape the provocative fragrance.

He'd lived like a monk for too long. It had been over a year since he'd had a physical relationship with anyone. He was a normal, healthy male and it was only natural that a woman as attractive and sweet-smelling as Caralie would affect him on a fundamental level.

He stood in relief when a square-faced man in a rumpled suit appeared and strode toward them purposefully. "Hi, I'm Boyd Farrell. I understand you wanted to speak to me."

Riley shook his hand. "I'm Riley Kincaid and this is Caralie Tracey. Her sister, Loretta, died in the Galveston hospital fire eight months ago."

"I'm sorry for your loss, Ms. Tracey," he said as he shook Caralie's hand.

"We'd like to find out where the investigation stands as of today," Caralie explained.

Farrell nodded. "Come to my office and we can talk more comfortably there."

They followed him through a labyrinth of corridors into a small office. The desk was buried beneath a blanket of paperwork and the room smelled of stale fast food and burned coffee.

"Please, have a seat." He gestured them to two folding chairs, then sank down behind the desk. "I'm afraid I don't have much information to share with you. The investigation has hit a brick wall."

"Can you tell us what you do know about the fire?" Riley asked.

"We know it was set intentionally. It was ignited in a storeroom in the maternity unit and spread quickly from there."

"But you haven't been able to find out who set it or why?" Caralie looked at him intently.

Farrell leaned back in his chair and raked a hand through his thin, sandy hair. "That's where we've hit a brick wall. You probably heard in the news media that immediately following the fire there was a kidnapping of one of the babies born that night. Initially we thought the two incidents were linked, but they weren't. We checked out hospital personnel, disgruntled ex-employees—all the usual potential suspects in a case like this. Unfortunately, our investigation turned up nothing."

Caralie opened her purse and withdrew what Riley recognized as the notes they'd discovered among Loretta's belongings the night before.

As Caralie explained to the sergeant about being out of the country and only just discovering about the fire and her sister's death in the last couple of days, Riley watched the play of emotions on her face.

She had one of the most expressive faces he'd ever

seen and in a flash she radiated her initial disbelief, her anger and finally her grief.

''Ms. Tracey,'' Sergeant Farrell began as he held the threatening notes she'd given him, ''I'm not sure how these are going to help our investigation. They aren't dated, so we have no way to be certain when your sister received them.''

''But she told me she got them just before the fire.''

''You spoke to her?''

Caralie flushed. ''No, she wrote me about the notes. Unfortunately, I didn't get those letters until just recently. Isn't it something you should follow up on?''

Boyd Farrell nodded, looking older and more tired than he had when they had first entered his office. ''Yes, and I'll do what I can. But I have to be honest with you—right now my priority and all my manpower are involved in trying to find some nut who has attempted to burn down four churches in the past two weeks.''

He stood, indicating an end to their discussion. ''I'd like to keep these and see what we can find out,'' he said, indicating the notes.

Caralie nodded. ''I'm staying with Mr. Kincaid for the moment. You'll be in touch?''

''Of course. Give the desk sergeant your phone number and I'll call you as soon as I have anything to report.''

Riley and Caralie were silent during the drive back to Houston. Riley felt her frustration rolling off her in waves, knew she was disappointed by what the arson investigator had told her.

"You okay?" he finally asked when the silence in the car had grown to stifling proportions.

She sighed and straightened in the seat. "Yes, I'm fine. I was just hoping to hear something different. I know it sounds crazy, but Loretta's death wouldn't be quite so horrible if I knew it was just a tragic accident."

"You were hoping he'd tell you the case had been solved and the fire had absolutely nothing to do with your sister."

She looked at him. "That's exactly what I was hoping."

"Okay, that didn't happen, so we move on to our next step. We'll stop in at Tommy's Tavern and see if anyone there can give us any information about where Loretta went after she quit working there."

As Riley drove toward Tommy's Tavern, he wondered again if his mother was right. Was he a fool to help Caralie? Should he instead be readying himself for a custody battle with her? Or was he following a fool's instincts, hoping that if he helped her find the answers to her sister's death, she would be so grateful she'd forget about taking Kaycee away from him?

TOMMY'S TAVERN WAS exactly the kind of place Caralie expected Loretta to have worked in—raucous, seedy and filled with enough testosterone to fuel a major-league football game.

Instinctively she moved closer to Riley as they

strode through the smoky, noisy interior toward the bar. The bartender was a big, burly man, his huge biceps decorated with colorful tattoos. He eyed them expressionlessly as they approached.

"Is the manager in?" Riley asked.

"I'm Tommy, the owner, manager, bartender and bouncer. What can I do for you?" Although his tone was not overtly unfriendly, neither was it particularly inviting.

"You remember a woman who used to work for you by the name of Loretta Tracey?"

"Maybe...maybe not." Tommy met Riley's gaze unflinchingly.

"Please...I'm Loretta's sister." Caralie stepped forward. "She died in a fire eight months ago and I'm trying to reconstruct the last year of her life. Please, if we could just ask you a few questions."

"You look like her," Tommy said after a long moment. "So...what do you want to know?"

"How long did she work for you?" Caralie asked.

"Not half long enough." Tommy grabbed a towel and swiped the countertop. "She was one of the best bartenders I've ever had. Worked here maybe three or four months before she moved on to greener pastures."

"'Greener pastures'? Where did she go?"

Tommy frowned. "Don't know for sure. She was doing a lot of volunteer work for Michael Monroe in his last election. His campaign headquarters was just down the street. Anyway, Loretta comes in here one day and says she quits because her luck has changed and she's never gonna have to worry about making money again.''

''That's it? She didn't say anything more?'' As Tommy shook his head, Caralie fought against overwhelming frustration. The mystery of Loretta appeared to be deepening and no answers seemed easily forthcoming.

''Maybe we should check with this Michael Monroe,'' Caralie said, once she and Riley had left Tommy's Tavern.

''Michael Monroe is the city Mayor of Houston. I'm not sure he'd know anything about a woman who volunteered for his campaign months ago.''

''We can't stop here,'' Caralie protested.

She warmed beneath Riley's supportive smile. ''Okay, then the next stop is Monroe's office...right after we grab something for lunch.''

They ate at a Mexican restaurant. The interior held little ambience but the service was great and the burritos terrific. Conversation halted between them as they focused on their plates. When they were finished, they headed toward Mayor Monroe's office.

In the plush downtown office they were greeted by a receptionist who explained to them that Mr. Monroe was in meetings for the remainder of the day.

''Could you give him a message for me?'' Caralie asked.

The receptionist, a platinum blonde with a million-dollar smile and a breast-size equivalent, nodded, although her attention was not focused on Caralie, but on Riley. Riley returned the woman's smile and Caralie swore she could hear the blonde purr.

"Tell him I'd like to speak to him about Loretta Tracey. She worked on his campaign. I'm her sister, Caralie."

"Why don't you write it all down," the woman replied. Not taking her eyes off Riley, she handed Caralie a memo pad and a pen.

Fighting a purely irrational irritation, Caralie quickly penned the information, then handed the pad back to the receptionist. "Thank you for your time," she said thinly.

"No problem... Anytime." She batted her lashes at Riley, who reacted like a typical male, his chest seeming to expand and his posture becoming a little straighter beneath her flirtatious gaze.

"I suppose that's the kind of woman that gained you your reputation," Caralie said when they were once again in the car traveling toward their next destination—Loretta's old apartment.

"What's that supposed to mean?"

She shrugged. "I just imagine you miss those days of wild adventure and nights of mindless sex."

A burst of rich laughter escaped him, further irritating Caralie. "Caralie, I have never in my life indulged in mindless sex." He gazed at her, his lips upturned in a smile, but his eyes radiating a dangerous certainty. "When I make love to a woman, I want both of us to be intensely aware of each sensation, every moment."

The flush that swept over Caralie began at her toes and slowly worked its way to her face. She averted her gaze, unable to maintain eye contact with him. It had been silly of her to open this particular can of worms. She didn't care whom he slept with or how intensely he made love.

At Loretta's old apartment they spoke to the landlady and Loretta's next-door neighbor. Sebastian, the neighbor, spoke fondly of Loretta, his pale eyes radiating grief, but he was on his way out and they only talked to him for a moment. The landlady couldn't tell them anything about what Loretta had been doing and how she'd been paying for the luxurious apartment. She did tell them that the rent was paid in cash on the first of every month and there was no lease.

Their next stop was the Houston hospital, in an effort to speak to staff members who had been working at the Galveston facility on the night of the fire. The doctor who had delivered Kaycee wasn't in, but Caralie left a message with one of his nurses, explaining what they wanted and leaving Riley's phone number.

They did find a nurse who had been on duty that night. Edith Webster, a tall, stern woman in a traditional starched white nurse's uniform, explained to them that she had been working the nurses' station down the hall from the maternity rooms. "I was too far away from the elevator to see who was coming and going that night," she explained. "It was a crazy night, what with three women in labor and delivering within minutes of each other, then the chaos of the fire."

"Is there any other nurse who was working the maternity floor that night who might have seen who came and went into those rooms?" Riley asked.

Edith frowned thoughtfully. "You might try Louise Nelson. I think she was working in Maternity that night."

"Do you know where we might find her?" Caralie asked.

Edith looked at her watch. "She's probably on dinner break right now. She usually eats in the cafeteria downstairs. She's about twenty-four, skinny as a rail and has short brown hair. You shouldn't have any problem finding her. She'll be wearing a badge with her name."

"I feel like we're on a scavenger hunt and somebody is hoarding all the goodies we're supposed to collect," Caralie said a moment later as she and Riley rode the elevator down to the cafeteria.

"Yeah, and the only thing we have on our list to collect is answers."

Caralie rubbed the center of her forehead, where a small ache lightly pounded. "I just can't believe that Loretta didn't tell anyone what was going on in her life. Surely she had a best friend—somebody she confided in."

"If she did have a best friend, we'll find her." Riley reached out and placed a hand on Caralie's shoulder. She wondered at how his simple touch could be both comforting and uncomfortable.

Comforting in that it was a reminder that she wasn't in this alone, that he intended to help her seek until they finally found some answers. Uncomfortable in that she longed to feel his arms wrap around her, hold her close against his chest; longed to nuzzle his neck where the sexy scent of his cologne seemed to originate.

He dropped his hand as the elevator dinged and the doors whooshed open. Caralie felt a mixture of relief and regret at the absence of his touch.

They found Louise Nelson at a table in the corner. She sat alone, thumbing through a magazine as she ate a salad. She looked up as they approached, her eyes a startling bright blue.

"Edith Webster said we might find you here," Caralie explained. "This is Riley Kincaid and I'm Caralie Tracey. We'd like to ask you some questions about the Galveston hospital fire."

"What kind of questions?" Her eyes narrowed, radiating anxiety and a touch of what Caralie thought might be fear.

"Loretta, my sister was the maternity patient who died in the fire. We think the fire might have been set intentionally to harm her."

Louise shoved her salad aside and gestured them to join her at the table. "The day after the fire we were all interviewed and I told the police everything I knew. I don't know what else you want to know."

"Did Loretta have any visitors that night?" Caralie leaned toward Louise, who looked fragile enough to be blown away by a small gust of wind. "Did you see anyone suspicious in or near her room?"

Louise shook her head. "Nobody who looked suspicious, but she did have a visitor."

"Who?" Adrenaline pumped through Caralie.

"I don't know who it was, but I can tell you it was a young woman."

"You remember what she looked like?" Riley asked.

Louise frowned. "Only vaguely. She looked really young and had long pale blond hair and I think I heard your sister call her 'Goldilocks.'" Louise flushed with obvious embarrassment. "You probably think I'm nuts, but I swear that's what Loretta called her."

"No, I don't think you're nuts," Caralie replied softly. "Is there anything else...anything at all you can tell us?"

Louise shrugged and offered Caralie a sympathetic smile. "Sorry, I can't think of anything else."

"And you didn't hear any of the conversation between Loretta and this 'Goldilocks'?"

She hesitated, a frown tugging her thin eyebrows closer together. "I was so busy that night. We were horribly understaffed and I was on the end of a double shift." She rubbed her slender hands together as if washing them beneath a faucet. "I remember one thing. I heard your sister say something about meeting 'Goldilocks' at Chubbie's after your sister got out of the hospital."

"'Chubbie's'?"

"It's a popular diner on the south side of town," Riley explained.

"That's it," Louise said as she stood. "That's all I know and now it's time for me to get back to work."

"Thank you for all your help," Caralie said as she stood also.

Louise nodded, her eyes glimmering with a hint of emotion. "I'm sorry about your sister. I feel responsible. When the fire broke out there was such pandemonium. I tried...but I couldn't get to her in time."

Impulsively Caralie stepped forward and embraced the thin woman, who trembled with suppressed emotion. "It's all right," Caralie said gently. "I'm sure you did all you could." She released Louise and with a curt nod the nurse headed for the elevator.

Twilight edged its way across the sky as they drove toward Riley's mother's house to pick up Kaycee. Caralie leaned wearily against the seat, watching the approach of another night.

"So, where do we go from here?" Riley asked as he pulled up in front of his mother's home. He unbuckled his seat belt and turned to face her.

"I'm not sure. I was hoping to get something more concrete to work with."

"I know you're disappointed, but we didn't come up totally empty-handed. Maybe this 'Goldilocks' is a regular down at Chubbie's and we'll be able to find out something about her." He frowned, the gesture only increasing his attractiveness. "Unless, of course, Louise is mistaken about the name. It sounds pretty odd."

"Not really. Loretta often nicknamed people in her life with fairy-tale names." Caralie smiled, remembering that particular quirk from when they had been children. "Most of the social workers were various witches and our best friends were Snow White and Sleeping Beauty—twin girls two years younger than me.''

''In this particular case, it's too bad Loretta didn't call the woman by her real name instead of a nickname. With a real name she might be easier to find.'' Riley opened his car door. ''You want to come in?''

Caralie shook her head. ''I'll just wait here.''

As Riley disappeared into the house, Caralie stared out at the darkening sky. She felt as if she'd swallowed a dark cloud. A sense of desolation swept over her as she thought over the day. So many people they'd spoken to, and still no answers about Loretta's life before the fire. Loretta had been a lost soul, like their mother before them.

When Riley reappeared, carrying a sleeping Kaycee in his arms, Caralie again vowed to herself that she would give the little girl all the love, all the nurturing and security that she and her sister had never had.

Kaycee didn't awaken as Riley buckled her into the infant seat. He tossed her stuffed animal onto the seat next to her, then got back behind the wheel. ''Mom said she refused to take a nap all afternoon, then fell asleep just a few minutes before we arrived. She'll probably sleep through most of the night.''

''I don't think I'll have any trouble sleeping through the night, either,'' Caralie said.

''It has been a long day,'' he agreed.

They fell silent for the remainder of the ride back to his house. Once there, Riley carried Kaycee up the back staircase that led into the second-story apartment and took her right to the nursery. Offering to make a pot of coffee, Caralie went into the kitchen.

She'd decided the first time she'd been in Riley's house that his kitchen was her favorite room. Although small and functional, it had an intimate coziness provided by the hunter-green and burgundy wallpaper border and the rich wood cabinets and round oak table.

The room radiated an aura of domesticity that was appealing, from the bib hanging over the back of the high chair, to the collection of plush toys that had somehow found a home on the shelf next to the telephone.

Within minutes the fragrance of fresh hot coffee filled the air. Caralie poured two cups, then sat down to wait for Riley. She tried not to think of him in with Kaycee, rubbing her little back, soothing her into pleasant dreams with his rumbly deep voice. Caralie didn't want to think about the fact that Riley seemed like a good father. "Hmm, that coffee smells good," Riley said as he came into the kitchen.

Caralie nodded. "This is one of the few luxuries I missed when I was in Africa—freshly brewed coffee."

Riley sank down across from her and cupped his mug with his hands. "Must have been tough, the kind of deprivation you had to live with over there."

"I had to make some adjustments, but for the most part it was an experience I'm glad I had."

"Do you plan on going back to work there?" He asked the question with a studied nonchalance, but Caralie suspected her answer was extremely important to him, especially if she managed to win custody of his daughter.

"No, we won't be going back." Caralie paused for a moment and took a sip of her coffee, then continued. "The last two years have been sort of a transitional period for me. Now I feel like it's time I started building something permanent."

"Are you going to work?"

She knew what he was after—ammunition that would help him when the custody fight began—but she didn't intend to give him any leverage. "I've got some money put aside so I won't have to for a little while. I want to be a full-time mother. Eventually I'd like to go back to school and get my nursing degree, but that would be several years down the line."

"Have you thought about where you'll start to build this new life?"

She smiled at him, knowing he worried about any distance she might put between him and his daughter. "Not really, but Houston looks like as good a place as any."

"I won't go down without one hell of a fight, you know," he warned her.

She nodded, knowing that as crazy as it seemed, she'd be disappointed in him if he didn't give her one hell of a fight.

A loud crash rent the air, followed by the faint tinkling of falling glass. Caralie dropped her cup, sloshing coffee onto the table. Riley jumped out of his chair. "What the hell!" he exclaimed. "It sounded like it came from the studio."

Caralie raced after him as he left the apartment

and went running down the stairs. Her heart thudded wildly, making her chest ache with trepidation. ''Everything looks all right,'' she ventured, eyeing the studio, which appeared normal.

Riley opened the door to the reception area and flipped on the light. He took two steps into the room and froze, Caralie crashing into his back.

The front-plate glass window was shattered. Thousands of shards littered the floor, glittering in the overhead light. Cool night air poured in through the broken pane.

Amid the slivers of glass was Kaycee's toy kitty, its neck cut open and the stuffing grotesquely pulled out. A small tag hung around one of its paws.

''I left it in the car,'' Riley said as he bent and picked it up. ''When I carried Kaycee in to bed, the cat was in the back seat.'' His features hardened ominously as he read the note attached to the furry foot.

''Wha-what does it say?'' Caralie asked in fear.

He looked at her, his eyes dark as night, stormy with suppressed emotion. ''It says, 'Curiosity killed the cat.' ''

Chapter Five

''Kaycee!'' The name exploded from Riley. He turned and raced back up the stairs. Caralie followed, her heart pounding in terror. Surely somebody hadn't managed to get into the house and harm the baby.

There were only two ways into the upstairs apartment, up the studio stairs or through the back door in the kitchen. Surely she and Riley would have heard anyone who tried to get in either door.

Riley stopped short in the doorway of the nursery and Caralie halted next to him, her relief whooshing out of her in a huge sigh. Kaycee remained safely sleeping, a thumb tucked securely in her rosebud mouth.

''Thank God,'' Riley murmured. For a moment he leaned against the doorjamb, as if his intense relief had stolen all his strength. He drew a deep breath, walked over to the crib and picked up his daughter. She didn't awaken but snuggled against him, her body conforming to his with an easy familiarity that caused an arrow of yearning to shoot through Caralie.

"I'll put her in the playpen in the studio," he said softly. "I don't want to leave her up here all alone."

She nodded and followed him downstairs. Once Kaycee was settled in the playpen, Riley and Caralie went back into the small reception area. "I need to call the police," he said, his jaw clenching and unclenching in what Caralie knew had to be anger.

"Do you have a broom? I could start sweeping up the mess," she offered.

"In the closet there," he told her, then picked up the phone to call the police.

Once the call had been made, Riley grabbed a second broom and together they worked in silence to clean up the broken glass.

They discovered a heavy concrete brick, which had obviously been heaved at the window to shatter it. They left the brick where it had landed for the police to see.

Within minutes a patrol car had arrived and two uniformed officers surveyed the damage. "You see who threw the block?" the dark-haired officer asked Riley.

"No, we were upstairs and heard the crash," Riley explained.

"You know anyone who might want to do something like this to you?" the older of the two officers asked.

"Nasty piece of work," the other observed as he looked at the tortured stuffed animal.

"We spent the day asking some people questions about a hospital fire that happened in Galveston eight months ago," Riley said. "It would appear somebody didn't like our questions.'' He looked at Caralie, his expression inscrutable.

''I'd say it would be wise to leave the investigation to the professionals,'' the older officer observed as he began to fill out his report.

As Riley and the two cops talked, Caralie went back to work sweeping up the remainder of the glass. Who had done this? Who was responsible? It frightened her to think that somebody they must have talked to today had felt threatened enough to follow them here and try to intimidate them.

Not only was she frightened, but as she looked at the empty space where the window had been, a surge of guilt welled up inside her. What had she gotten Riley into? What had she gotten herself into?

The officers hung around long enough to finish their report, then left after indicating Riley should call if there were any further problems.

With Caralie's help, Riley nailed a piece of plywood across the yawning gap in the wall. He hit the nails with more force than necessary as his jaw knotted and bunched in his anger.

Caralie didn't blame him for being angry. He'd offered to help her, but he hadn't bargained on a shattered plate glass and a threat of danger.

''There, that should hold it until morning when I can get a glass company out here,'' he said as he drove in the last nail with a thunderous bang.

''I'll be glad to pay for the replacement window,'' Caralie said as she sank into one of the chairs, with the mauled stuffed cat in her hands.

"Don't be ridiculous," he returned irritably. "My insurance will take care of most of the cost."

"I shouldn't have involved you in this," she said quietly, her gaze fixed on the ruined animal. She looked at him regretfully. "I'll pack up and leave first thing in the morning."

Riley put his hammer away and sat down next to her. "So, you're ready to quit...give up? You don't want to find out exactly what happened to Loretta?" His words were clipped, his tone not masking his simmering anger.

"Of course not," Caralie replied with an anger of her own. But the feeling couldn't sustain itself under the enormous guilt she felt as she stared at Kaycee's mutilated toy. "But it isn't fair for you to get caught up in all this. This really isn't your problem. It has nothing to do with you."

Riley's anger sprang loose. He shot out of the chair and turned to face her. "How dare you decide what has to do with me and what doesn't! We're talking about the mother of my daughter—a woman I once cared about."

He swiped a hand through his hair and drew an audible deep breath. "It's quite obvious by what happened here that we made somebody very uncomfortable with our questions today."

Caralie nodded. "I don't want to bring trouble to your doorstep." She fought back a shiver. "I had no idea this might happen." She looked at the boarded-over window.

"I don't intend to stop seeking answers now. With you or without you, I'm digging deeper." He gestured to the stuffed animal in Caralie's hand. "Whoever did that made a big mistake. They made their threat by destroying something my daughter loved, and for that, they'll pay."

He sighed, and she watched as he forced a smile. "In fact, I have a feeling we'll all pay in the morning when she wakes up and doesn't have her favorite kitty. Come on, let's go back upstairs and finish our coffee. We need to do a little brainstorming about what our next move is going to be."

His use of the words "we" and "our" warmed Caralie. She'd been frightened by the latest turn of events, and was grateful that she wasn't in this alone.

A flare of renewed guilt momentarily burned in the pit of her stomach as she followed Riley back upstairs, with Kaycee cradled in his arms. She was grateful it was Riley and not David who stood beside her in this particular set of circumstances, and the thought made her feel like a traitor.

If she were tending a sick child, she'd want David with his gentle touch and compassionate heart beside her. But in this situation, with the winds of danger blowing so near, she wanted Riley with his broad shoulders and sinewy strength. She needed Riley with his flashing eyes and passionate desire to get to the truth.

When Kaycee was once again settled and sleeping peacefully in her crib, Riley poured them each a fresh cup of coffee and Caralie sat at the table. Before he joined her, he grabbed a notepad from a drawer.

"I think the first thing we need to do is make a list of everyone we spoke to today," he began.

''A list of potential suspects,'' Caralie explained.

''Exactly.'' It took them only moments to write the names of the people they had contacted. Riley studied the list, a frown wrinkling his brow. ''But you know this isn't complete,'' he said.

''What do you mean?'' She returned his frown in confusion.

''Anyone could have overheard us in Tommy's Tavern or when we spoke to Louise in the hospital cafeteria. A dozen other people could have seen the note you left for Michael Monroe.''

''Are you trying to cheer me up?'' Caralie asked dryly.

He flashed her a quicksilver smile. ''No, just making sure we both understand the reality of the situation. We don't have a lot to go on, but we have a start. Whoever is responsible made a mistake tonight.''

''What kind of a mistake?''

''By warning us off, they let us know we got too close.'' He tapped the paper in front of him. ''And we got too close by talking to these people.''

Caralie stared at the list glumly. So many names. Tommy, Edith, Louise. Michael Monroe's receptionist, Loretta's landlady and Sebastian. And that didn't count anyone who might have overheard their questioning. ''So, where do we go from here?'' she asked.

''To bed,'' he replied. ''It's been a long day. Let's get some sleep and finish this brainstorming in the morning.'' He drained his coffee cup and stood to carry it to the sink.

Caralie did the same, realizing she was exhausted. Riley was right. It had been a long day and she'd had little sleep the night before. There was nothing more to be gained tonight.

Riley turned off the coffeepot and together they left the kitchen and started down the hallway toward their bedrooms.

Caralie stopped him at her doorway and placed a hand on his broad chest. "Riley, I know you've said you're doing all this for Kaycee, because someday she'll want some answers. I just wanted to tell you again that no matter what your reasons for helping me, I appreciate it." Self-consciously she dropped her hand from his chest, her fingers tingling from the brief physical contact.

He reached out and tucked a strand of her hair behind her ear. It was an intimate act, an evocative one that seemed to change the consistency of the air around them.

Caralie's breath caught in her chest as he gazed at her. "You aren't accustomed to having people in your life to help you." It wasn't a question, but rather a statement of fact.

She hesitated, then shook her head, finding it difficult to speak as he took a step closer to her.

Again his hand went to her hair, this time caressing the length of it. "This is one thing you don't have to do alone, Caralie." His voice was hypnotically low and smooth. "We're going to figure this out. Together we'll find out what happened to Loretta and you'll have the peace you seem to need to find."

"Thank you." The words had barely escaped her

when he dipped his head and covered her lips with his.

She hadn't anticipated the kiss, had no time to erect mental or physical defenses against it. His mouth was warm and soft, sending rivulets of pleasure shimmering up and down her back.

All too quickly it was over. He ended the kiss and stepped back from her. "Good night," he murmured. His voice had a husky edge. Without waiting for her response, he turned and disappeared down the hall into his own bedroom.

Caralie stood there for a long moment. Confusion and surprise held her in place. She reached up and gently brushed her mouth with her fingertips.

Why? Why had he kissed her? What insanity had possessed him? And why...oh, why, had his kiss managed to touch her clear down to her toes?

David's sweet, gentle kisses had never had much effect on her. Of course, she hadn't kissed David often. Their relationship was based more on friendship and respect, and had little to do with passion or physical attraction.

She went into her bedroom and closed the door behind her, as if in doing so she could shut out the sensation of his lips against hers.

As she changed out of her clothes and into her nightgown, she considered what madness might have driven Riley to kiss her.

He was a man who thrived on adrenaline, who had made his living by creating photographic chronicles of danger. The adrenaline flow produced by danger must be a lot like the surge that accompanied passion. Yes, that was the logical explanation for his action.

Now, all she had to do was try to figure out an equally logical explanation for her swift, intense response to the kiss.

IT WAS JUST BEFORE NINE the next morning when Kaycee awakened Riley with her usual yell for attention. He looked at his clock in surprise, unable to remember the last time he'd slept so late. Apparently Caralie was still in bed, as exhausted as he had been from the turmoil of the night before.

As Kaycee ate a piece of toast, Riley phoned a glass company, and was pleased when the company said they could send someone out immediately.

Thirty minutes later, the workmen arrived and Riley moved Kaycee down to the playpen in the studio so he could keep an eye on her and survey the job being done.

Caralie's bedroom door remained closed and Riley hoped the work on the window didn't awaken her from much-needed sleep. She probably hadn't slept well since receiving Loretta's letters a week ago.

He sat on a chair in the doorway that separated the studio from the reception area, alternating his attention between the men at work and his daughter at play. As he sat, his thoughts returned to that moment in the hallway the night before.

He had no idea why he'd kissed Caralie, other than the fact that he'd wanted to taste those lips of hers from the moment she'd walked through his front door.

The kiss had been a mistake—a terrible mistake in that it had awakened a part of him that had been dormant for a very long time. For the past eight months, he had been less man, more father. His every waking thought had been on how to meet Kaycee's needs; and in the process of wanting to be good enough for his daughter, he'd neglected pieces of himself.

He was aware of how foolish it would be to become entangled with Caralie Tracey. She had her future mapped out before her. She'd marry her David and they'd build a life together.

In the worst case scenario, she'd have custody of Kaycee. In his best-case scenario, he'd have Kaycee and would agree to allow Caralie occasional visits with the little girl.

However, even knowing how foolish it would be to get emotionally or physically involved with Caralie, he couldn't stop thinking about the sweet heat of her lips, the honeyed taste of passion that had resided there.

As she'd returned his kiss, he'd wanted to back her into the bedroom, stretch out on the crisp white sheets and lose himself in her. Somehow, she touched him in a place nobody else had, since— He stopped his mental process right there.

He shifted position on the chair, uncomfortable with the direction of his thoughts. His mother was right. For months she'd been telling him he should be dating; that a healthy, fulfilled man made a happier, better father.

He'd done a lot of wild, crazy things in his life,

but sleeping with Caralie, allowing himself any kind of personal relationship with her, would be beyond wild and crazy. It would be utter madness. Hell, he still hadn't decided if he actually liked the woman or not.

Kaycee fussed unhappily in the playpen. She pulled herself up to stand and tossed out one of her toys. She'd been fussy since first waking up, and Riley knew the reason why: She missed her favorite kitty.

Riley's stomach knotted with anger as he thought of what someone had done to the stuffed animal. Eventually he hoped he got an opportunity to extract a modicum of revenge from the responsible party.

He'd agreed to help Caralie find the answers to Loretta's death for several reasons. Initially it had been in an effort to buy himself time, perhaps with the subconscious notion that he could ingratiate himself with her and she would drop the idea of a custody battle. He'd seen her need for answers in her eyes, and now his own need burned in his heart.

Within an hour, the empty window had been replaced with a brand-new plate glass and the workmen had moved on to their next job. Riley took Kaycee back upstairs, noting with surprise that Caralie's bedroom door was still closed and no sound came from within.

He placed Kaycee on the living-room floor and gave her a handful of toys. While Caralie slept, Riley figured it was as good a time as any to take down the Christmas tree.

As he removed the soft, fabric ornaments and tried

to put them in storage boxes, Kaycee helped, making the process longer and more complicated, but much more fun.

"Riley?" His mother's voice rang out from the back door.

"In here, Mom," Riley replied.

Margaret appeared in the doorway, half out of breath. "I can't wait for you to find a real house so I don't have to climb a set of stairs every time I want to visit you," she exclaimed. She barely paused. "Hi, sweet poppet," she said as she scooped Kaycee up in her arms. "Are you helping Daddy?"

"Da-da-da!" Kaycee laughed and handed her grandma one of the colorful ornaments.

"What are you doing in this part of town?" Riley asked. Terrific, just what he needed. He hadn't mentioned to his mother the day before that Caralie was actually staying with him. All he needed was for Caralie to stumble out of her bedroom with her hair sleep-tousled and wearing her robe.

"I had a sweater to return to the store. Your Aunt Jennifer has all her taste in her mouth. She sent me the gaudiest creation I've ever seen in my life." Margaret sat on the sofa, Kaycee in her lap. "Anyway, I thought while I was so close, I'd drop by."

Riley nodded, wondering how he could get his mother out of the place before Caralie emerged. Although he was a grown man, Margaret Kincaid had the ability to castigate him until he felt like a five-year-old instead of a thirty-year-old. He wasn't in the mood for it this morning.

"How did it go yesterday?" Margaret asked.

''When you picked up Kaycee you didn't say anything about what you found out. Did you learn anything new about the fire and Loretta's death?''

''Not really.'' Riley finished with the ornaments and began peeling off the strings of lights from the tree. ''Although we did learn that Loretta had a visitor at the hospital—a young woman. We're going to see if we can figure out exactly who she is. If she's a good friend of Loretta's, maybe she'll have some answers for us.''

Margaret frowned. ''I just hope you aren't getting too involved in all this, Riley. Have you contacted a lawyer yet?''

Riley shook his head. ''I haven't had time.''

''You'd better make time. You can be sure this Caralie person is doing all she can to dig up every piece of dirt from your past, and unfortunately, she'll have little trouble doing so.''

''Mom.'' Riley winced and cast a glance down the hallway, hoping Caralie couldn't hear the conversation. ''I'll take care of things. Don't you worry about it.''

''I have to worry about it,'' Margaret protested. She kissed the top of Kaycee's head. ''She's my grandbaby, Riley. I don't want to lose her.''

Riley heard the choked emotion in his mother's voice. He set the string of lights on the floor and joined his mom on the sofa. ''We aren't going to lose her. Even if Caralie somehow wins custody, she won't take Kaycee away from us completely.''

''How do you know? What do you really know about this woman?'' Margaret demanded.

I know her mouth tastes like honey and her hair is soft as silk. I know her scent drives me wild and her breasts would fit perfectly into my palms. Riley stood, irritated by his wayward thoughts. ''I don't know that much about her,'' he admitted. ''But I know she cares about Kaycee and she wouldn't deprive Kaycee of our love.'' He hoped—prayed—that what he said was true.

The back door opened, then closed. ''Who could that be?'' Riley started toward the kitchen, then halted as Caralie appeared in the doorway, a shopping bag in hand.

''Oh...am I interrupting?'' she asked hesitantly. Her face flushed a becoming pink. ''Perhaps I should have knocked.''

''No, it's fine. Caralie, this is my mother, Margaret. Mom, this is Caralie.''

''How do you do,'' Margaret said and Riley saw her arms tighten slightly around Kaycee.

''It's nice to meet you, Mrs. Kincaid,'' Caralie replied, looking distinctly ill at ease.

''Please, call me Margaret. After all, we are sort of family in this mishmash mess.''

Caralie nodded and opened the shopping bag. ''I had to go to three different stores to finally find one,'' she said as she withdrew a stuffed cat exactly like the one that had been destroyed.

As it came into view, Kaycee bounced up and down on Margaret's lap, her little hands opening and closing in the nonverbal expression of want. Caralie laughed and gave the animal to the little girl.

Warmth spread through Riley as he watched Kaycee hug the kitty. It touched him that Caralie had obviously gotten up early and gone in search of the toy she knew Kaycee would miss. "Thanks," he muttered, his voice sounding oddly hoarse to his ears.

"What happened to her other one?" Margaret asked.

"It got ruined," Riley hurriedly told her before Caralie could say anything. "I...uh... I tried to wash it and it fell apart." Riley wasn't one for lying, but he didn't want his mother to know what had actually happened to the stuffed animal. She would only worry, and she had already had nearly a lifetime of worrying about Riley and his escapades.

Margaret rolled her eyes. "I suppose you just threw it into the machine willy-nilly, without using the 'delicate' cycle."

Riley smiled sheepishly, but didn't answer.

Margaret straightened her back, her gaze moving from Riley to Caralie. "Let's get down to the real brass tacks of this situation," she said. "So, tell me, Caralie, do you really intend to fight for custody and break my son's heart?"

"Mom!" Riley protested as Caralie's face flamed with color once again.

"No, it's all right," Caralie said. "I'm hoping nobody will have to end up with a broken heart," she replied. "But to answer the first part of your question, yes. I intend to fight for custody. It's what Loretta wanted."

"How do you know what your sister wanted?" Margaret asked. "From what I've been told, you've been out of the country."

''My sister wrote me and told me if anything happened to her, she didn't want the father to have custody, she wanted me to.''

''But she must have had a change of heart,'' Margaret objected. ''She not only put Riley's name on the birth certificate, but she also left his name and address as her next of kin to contact in case of an emergency.''

''Look,'' Riley said, deciding there had been enough discussion on this particular topic. ''None of us can know for sure exactly what Loretta wanted at the time of her death, and we aren't going to settle it by arguing among ourselves.''

He looked at his mother, then at Caralie. ''Maybe we'll know better when we learn more about what was going on in Loretta's life before the night of the fire. And speaking of that—'' he gazed at his mother again ''—could you watch Kaycee for a couple of hours tonight? We have a hot lead to follow up on.''

''Of course. You know I'm always willing and ready to baby-sit her. In fact, if you'd like, I could just take her with me now and you can pick her up later, after you've followed your hot lead.''

Riley hesitated. On the one hand he felt each moment he spent with Kaycee had suddenly become more precious, but he also knew his mother wanted as much time with her as possible.

''Okay,'' he agreed. ''If you go ahead and take her, Caralie and I can get back to work on hunting down some more answers.''

Besides, he thought, the faster they solved the

mystery of Loretta, the faster Caralie would be out of his house. And with the memory of their kiss still lingering in his mind, he had a feeling that would be best for both of them.

Chapter Six

Under different circumstances, Caralie might have enjoyed dinner at Chubbie's. The restaurant was huge, the motif strictly fifties. Riley and Caralie were led to one of the high-backed leather booths by a waitress in a white blouse and bright pink poodle skirt. A poster of Fabian smiled down at them as they opened the menus.

"Can you give us a few minutes?" Riley asked the waitress as she set ice water in front of them.

"Sure," she agreed easily, then hurried off to tend to another table.

Instead of scanning the menu, Caralie gazed at the other diners, searching for the elusive blonde her sister had named "Goldilocks."

The restaurant apparently catered to a diverse clientele. A middle-aged conservative couple sat at one of the black-and-chrome round tables, while the table next to them was occupied by a young man with a Mohawk haircut, wearing a nose ring, and his companion, a purple-haired woman with colorful diamond shapes painted around her eyes.

"I suddenly feel very old," Caralie said.

Riley followed her gaze, then grinned. "Ah, youth... It's wasted on the young."

Caralie closed her menu and once again surveyed the surroundings, then sighed. "You realize we're probably on a wild-goose chase," she said.

"Maybe," he agreed easily. "But we had to eat, so we might as well eat here and see if this 'Goldilocks' shows up."

Caralie nodded and opened her menu once again. Earlier in the afternoon she had called Louise Nelson at the hospital and had gotten as complete a description of the young woman who'd visited Loretta as the nurse could remember.

Caralie had a fairly good mental picture of what she thought "Goldilocks" looked like, but the image would do no good if the young woman didn't appear.

She looked up at Riley, who was studying the crowd just as she had done minutes before. "What happens if she doesn't come in tonight?"

"Then we come back here and eat tomorrow night. And if she doesn't come in tomorrow night, then we try again the next night."

Caralie smiled impishly. "And by the end of the week we'll both weigh eight hundred pounds from eating the fat-laden fare they have on the menu."

Riley laughed, the skin at the corners of his eyes crinkling attractively and his dimple dancing in his left cheek. "Don't tell me you're one of those fastidious women who only eat bran and lettuce."

Caralie smiled, then sobered. "Seriously, Riley,

we must be crazy to think that eight months after the fact, this same woman will show up here,'' she said.

He nodded somberly. ''But, there are several things to consider. According to Louise, it was 'Goldilocks' who set this place for her meeting with Loretta. That implies that 'Goldilocks' felt a certain comfort level here, and that implies familiarity.'' He took a sip of his water, then continued. ''This is a neighborhood place, generally frequented by the same crowd night after night.''

''How do you know that?'' she asked curiously.

''Look around. Notice how the waitresses appear to know everyone...that the customers nod and smile at each other with familiarity.''

Caralie gazed around once again, noting that he was right. ''You're very observant.''

He smiled. ''For years that was part of my job.''

''And you liked what you did? The travel...the danger?''

He hesitated before answering. She tried not to notice how handsome he looked. His long-sleeved gold shirt emphasized matching flecks in his dark eyes. A five o'clock shadow dusted his cheeks and chin, giving him a slightly rakish, rather dangerous quality. His hair was carelessly tousled and looked feather soft.

''I loved what I did while I was doing it,'' he replied thoughtfully. ''It was what I needed. I was good at it because I didn't care.''

Caralie looked at him curiously. What an odd way to put it. '''Didn't care'?''

He averted his gaze from hers. ''It was during a

time in my life when I didn't want to have time to think…time to feel. The danger and the excitement made it impossible to think of anything else but the work.'' He looked at her again, his dark gaze warning her off. ''And that's enough about me. Tell me about this David you eventually plan to marry.''

Interesting. Caralie sensed a mystery in Riley's past. She sighed. She had more than enough mystery with Loretta's death. She didn't want to attempt to delve into another one. ''There's not much to tell. He's a doctor. He's quiet and serious and committed to helping the underprivileged both in other countries and here.''

''Sounds like a real saint,'' Riley observed.

Caralie looked at him sharply, wondering if she only imagined the slight sarcasm in his voice. ''He's a good man.''

The waitress appeared once again at their booths.

''I'll have a double cheeseburger, an order of fries and a chocolate shake,'' Caralie said, then smiled at Riley. ''Lettuce and bran, indeed.''

He grinned. ''I'll have the same,'' he told the waitress. ''Before you place our orders, can I ask you a question?''

The waitress shrugged and smiled easily. ''Sure. As long as you don't ask me the secret ingredient in the special hamburger sauce.''

''We're looking for a young woman who supposedly comes in here quite frequently. She has long pale blond hair.

''Fairly young? Big blue eyes?''

''Yes.'' Caralie leaned forward eagerly. ''That

sounds like her. Do you know her name or where she lives?''

The waitress shook her head. ''Sorry, hon. I can tell you she likes her burgers plain and her fries extra crispy, but I don't know her name or her address.''

''She comes in frequently?'' Riley asked.

Again the waitress shrugged. ''Pretty often—several times a month.''

''When was the last time she was in?''

''I don't know, maybe a week ago.'' There was a touch of impatience in the waitress's voice.

''Thanks for the information,'' Riley said.

She nodded and hurried away from their table. It took only minutes for her to return with their food.

As Riley and Caralie ate, their conversation remained light and pleasant. However, neither of them forgot the reason they were there. Both of them constantly scanned the crowd, looking for ''Goldilocks.''

''Your mother seems nice,'' Caralie said as she nibbled on the last of her fries.

''My mother is opinionated, stubborn and utterly maddening. But she loves me and so I forgive her for her faults.''

Caralie laughed. ''I have a feeling you probably inherited most of those same qualities from her.''

''I'll admit, I am a bit opinionated, and I have been known to be stubborn, but I absolutely refuse to admit to being maddening,'' he protested.

She shoved her plate aside and once again scrutinized the diners. As it grew later, more and more people were drifting in, but still not the woman they sought.

"Maybe we should talk to Sebastian again," she suggested. "When we spoke to him we didn't know anything about this 'Goldilocks,' so maybe we didn't ask the right questions."

"You could be right," Riley agreed. "It's possible he saw this woman coming and going from Loretta's apartment and didn't think it was important. We can go back tomorrow and ask him a few more questions."

Caralie nodded and took a drink of the rich chocolate shake. "Tell me what you know about the mayor, Michael Monroe."

Riley shrugged. "Not much. He's married, has two kids and gets his picture in the paper pretty often. Beyond that, I don't know much about him."

"I was surprised that he returned my call today."

"Yeah, too bad he had nothing to offer us."

"I'm not even sure he remembered exactly who Loretta was."

Riley smiled dryly. "Probably not, but he's a good politician and that's why he called you." He tensed, his gaze moving beyond Caralie.

She turned to see what had caught his attention. Their waitress was pointing toward the front door. Caralie's heart skipped a beat as she saw the young woman who had just entered the diner. Clad in a bulky blue sweater and a pair of tight blue jeans, she looked like a typical teenager.

However it was her hair that captured Caralie's attention. Golden blond, it tumbled over her shoulders and fell to the center of her back in big heavy curls. And she had big blue eyes, a heart-shaped face. Louise's description fit the woman perfectly.

"It's her," Caralie said urgently. "It's got to be her."

Riley slid out of the booth and started walking toward the woman. At that moment, the blonde saw the waitress pointing to her, then saw Riley advancing. Her eyes widened and utter panic washed over her face. Before Riley could reach her, she turned and fled out the door.

"Riley, get her!" Caralie yelled, unmindful of the curious stares from the other diners.

As Riley flew out the door in pursuit, Caralie fumbled in her purse and withdrew a twenty-dollar bill. She threw it on the table, then stumbled from the booth.

As she raced for the door her mind spun out of control. Why had Goldilocks run? Who was she and what did she have to hide? *Please, catch her, Riley,* she thought. *Catch her this time because I have a feeling we won't get a second chance.*

She left Chubbie's, darting out into the cool night air. Her gaze darted left...then right. Nothing. Nobody. The street was empty. She stood in front of the restaurant, wondering what had happened to Goldilocks—and more important what had happened to Riley.

RILEY RAN LIKE THE WIND, his chest aching from the unaccustomed exercise. Eight months of fatherhood and relatively easy living had taken their toll. He was out of shape.

He wished he could say the same thing for the woman he chased. She maintained the distance between them, her legs pumping in graceful rhythm. "Wait! I don't want to harm you!" Riley yelled. "I just want to ask you some questions!"

She didn't reply. She didn't look back, and she didn't slow down. Riley pushed himself harder, his heartbeat pounding in his ears, his lungs burning from the effort that slowly closed the distance between them.

He cursed inwardly as she rounded a corner, momentarily disappearing from view. Riley followed, his feet skidding to a halt when he saw the gang of street punks between him and Goldilocks.

"Help me!" she cried. "He tried to attack me."

"What are you? Some kind of pervert?" a big burly young man shouted as he advanced on Riley.

"I don't want any trouble," Riley said breathlessly. He never saw the punch coming. It landed in his solar plexus. Pain exploded. What little breath he had left whooshed out of him as he dropped to his knees.

Before he had time to recover, a boot landed in the small of his back. He careened forward, his chin meeting the pavement. As he fell, he was vaguely aware of the woman climbing into a taxi.

"This will teach you to mess with ladies," a deep voice said. Once again, pain erupted as a boot met Riley's ribs. He gasped once as consciousness wavered. With a sigh, he reached for the darkness that descended over him.

He had no idea how long he remained unconscious. When he opened his eyes he was still sprawled on the sidewalk, but he was alone. He smelled the concrete of the walk, tasted the slight tang of blood.

Tentatively, he sat up. Although his back and ribs were sore, he didn't think anything was broken. His chin throbbed and he swiped a hand across it, unsurprised to find blood; the meeting between his chin and the pavement had opened an old scar.

He pulled a handkerchief from his back pocket and pressed it against the wound, then stood and started the walk back to Chubbie's.

Pausing beneath a streetlight, he looked at his watch, surprised to discover that the entire incident had taken no more than a few minutes.

He saw Caralie standing in front of the restaurant, looking down the street in the opposite direction. She turned and saw him. Her eyes widened and a hand shot up to her mouth. She ran toward him.

''Riley...are you all right?'' She touched his cheek. ''What happened? You're bleeding.''

''I'm okay,'' he replied. ''She told a gang of guys at the corner that I tried to attack her. They defended her honor.'' With the handkerchief still pressed against his chin, he used his other hand to take Caralie's elbow. ''Come on, let's go home.''

Driving back to the house, he felt the adrenaline that had been his companion flee his body. Without its protective surge of energy, every muscle ached and his ribs and chin throbbed with dull intensity.

"I'll call my mother and ask her to keep Kaycee overnight," he said, once they were at the house. "There's no way I want to pick her up tonight in this condition and hear my mother rant and rave."

"When you're finished with the phone call, I want to take a look at that chin and your ribs," Caralie said, frowning. "Maybe we should have gone to the emergency room for X rays."

"That's not necessary. I've had broken ribs before and I'm fairly sure they aren't broken now—just bruised and sore." He picked up the phone and punched in his mother's number.

When he'd finished his call, Caralie gazed at him expectantly. "Take off your shirt," she said briskly. "I want to check those ribs and then we need to clean out that chin."

Riley unbuttoned his shirt, feeling oddly self-conscious beneath her dispassionate gaze. He removed the shirt and placed it on the back of the sofa, then stood still to allow Caralie to check him out.

Her fingertips were pleasantly cool against the heat of his flesh. He tensed at their erotic dance across his ribs. His breath caught in his throat as she traced each rib.

She moved behind him and looked at his back. "You already have a bruise here." She touched it lightly and he jumped and winced. She dropped her hand and stepped back in front of him. "Do you have a first-aid kit?"

"Yeah, under the sink in the kitchen."

She took him by the hand and led him into the kitchen, where she gestured to a chair at the table, then retrieved the first-aid kit.

Opening the tin box, she withdrew peroxide and cotton balls. She tilted his head back and eyed the wound. "Well, it's finally stopped bleeding. I suppose you'll be all right without stitches."

"It was an old scar. About once every two years or so it gets reopened," he explained as she dabbed it with a peroxide-soaked cotton ball. "Once it got reopened in a bar brawl in Mexico. I got hit in the chin and the guy saw all the blood and freaked out. He thought he'd shattered my jaw."

"Stop talking," she commanded. "You're making it more difficult than it has to be."

He closed his mouth. She had no idea just how difficult things were. He'd been rambling in an effort to keep his mind off her intimate nearness. She was tending him as a nurse, but he was responding to her as if she were all woman.

Her scent surrounded him—a touch of exotic flowers mingling with a hint of femininity. Her breath fanned his throat, a seductive warmth that aroused a responding heat deep inside him.

She appeared to be concentrating solely on cleaning the wound, completely unaware of her effect on him. He breathed a sigh of relief as she backed away. "There, that should do it," she said.

It wasn't until she averted her gaze from his and he noted the heightened color in her cheeks that he realized she wasn't as unaware as she'd appeared.

"And now what you need is a nice hot bath," she said.

"I don't take baths, I take showers," Riley replied.

"If you know what's good for you, you'll take a bath. Otherwise you'll be so sore you won't be able to get out of bed in the morning. I'll go start the water."

She disappeared from the kitchen. A moment later he heard the sound of the water running in the bathroom. A hot bath did sound good. But a cold shower was what he needed, he thought ruefully as he stood. Still, already he could feel his muscles tightening and knew she was right.

He wandered into the living room, which looked oddly bare without the Christmas tree and decorations. He tried to imagine how barren his life would be without Kaycee. The resulting image was too painful to contemplate.

Why couldn't Caralie leave things alone? Why did she have to show up here and destroy the peaceful, loving atmosphere he'd created for himself and his daughter?

He frowned, realizing what he was doing. He was consciously creating a heady dose of anger to counter the desire he felt for Caralie. At this realization, his building anger seeped away.

How could he blame Caralie for wanting Kaycee? Rationally, he couldn't, but when it came to his daughter his thoughts weren't rational, but rather, gut-wrenchingly emotional.

"Riley? The bath is ready." Caralie interrupted

his thoughts. "While you soak, I'll make us some hot tea."

"Thanks." He moved past her in the hallway and into the steamy bathroom. He grinned in surprise as he saw the bubbles in the water and smelled the faint scent of strawberries. It had been decades since he'd taken a bubble bath.

He shucked off his jeans and underwear and slid into the water, hissing in pleasure as the fragrant hot water surrounded him.

The water sluiced over his shoulders, easing kinked muscles. Not only could he not remember the last time he'd had a bath, he knew for certain he'd never gotten into a bubble bath drawn by a woman. It felt oddly intimate...domestic.

He leaned his head back against the cool porcelain and closed his eyes. Instantly his mind filled with a vision of Caralie, her hair loose and flowing down her back as she approached the tub, naked, her eyes gleaming.

He could almost feel her body against his, smell the fragrance of her perfume. He could see a picture of them, like a husband and wife, reveling in their pleasure of each other.

He snapped his eyes open and jerked his head up, refusing to allow the mental vision to advance further. He'd decided a long time ago that love wasn't in the cards for him. He'd loved once and the experience had nearly destroyed him. Kaycee had been an unexpected gift—one that had reminded him of all that was good and sweet in life. But, he had no desire to add any other woman to his life.

Once again he leaned his head back against the cool porcelain and closed his eyes, this time allowing all thoughts to drift away.

CARALIE'S HAND SHOOK slightly as she filled the teakettle with water and set it on the stove to boil. She sank into a chair at the table, then instantly stood and began to pace. Too many emotions swirled inside for her to sit still. She needed to keep moving and sort them out.

She was disappointed that Goldilocks had eluded them. She knew with gut certainty that the young woman wouldn't appear at Chubbie's again anytime soon. Why had she run? What was she afraid of? And did it have something to do with Loretta?

Getting out two cups and the tea bags, she thought of those moments when her fingers had run lightly across Riley's skin. Her fingertips tingled at the simple memory. His flesh had been as smooth as polished copper, but unlike metal, it had been warm to the touch.

She'd had to fight with herself to stop at his ribs. She'd wanted to run her hands across the wide expanse of his back, slide her fingers through his springy chest hair, feel the ripple of his muscles beneath the smooth surface.

How was it possible to love David—and yet want Riley? Why had she never felt this kind of mindless, intense longing for the man she eventually planned to marry?

The teakettle whistled and she jumped in surprise. She lowered the heat beneath the kettle to keep the water warm, then sank into a chair at the table, her burst of frantic energy spent.

Okay, she could admit to finding Riley extremely attractive on a physical level, but Riley would never be the kind of man who would make her feel emotionally safe. He was a player; a man who loved all women, but gave his heart to none exclusively. She knew his reputation and knew to steer clear of him.

''Whew, you were right. That was just what I needed.'' Riley came into the kitchen wearing only a pair of gray sweatpants. His hair was damp and he filled the air with the scent of minty soap and the underlying fragrance of strawberries.

Caralie stood and motioned him to the table. ''Sit down and I'll pour the tea.'' She wished he'd put a shirt on, covered his chest with material so she couldn't see it.

As he sat at the table, she poured their tea, then joined him there. ''I'm sorry, Riley, about tonight and you getting hurt.''

He smiled at her. ''You've got to stop apologizing for things that aren't your fault.''

''I can't help but feel partially responsible.''

''Well, stop it right now. I'm a big boy and I take responsibility for myself.'' He took a tentative sip of the hot tea.

''I guess we're back to square one,'' Caralie said, trying to keep her disappointment from her voice. ''I doubt if Goldilocks will go back to Chubbie's now that she knows we're looking for her.''

''I've got a little ace in the hole that just might help us.''

"What?" She eyed him curiously.

"As I was getting introduced to the fellow's boots, our prey hopped into a taxi and disappeared. However, it wasn't just any taxi...it was a Bowman's taxi."

"And that's your ace in the hole?"

He smiled. "Russ Bowman, the owner of the company owes me a huge favor. I'll call him first thing in the morning and I'll bet he can tell us exactly where his driver delivered Ms. Goldilocks."

"What did you ever do for Russ Bowman that he'd do such a favor for you?"

Riley grinned. "I photographed his kid."

Caralie looked at him dubiously. "You took pictures of his kid? That's it?"

"It was a little more complicated than it sounds. You see, Russ has the child from hell. A screaming, kicking, spitting, temper-tantrum-throwing child who gives new meaning to the term 'the terrible twos.'" Riley laughed and shook his head. "It was a nightmare. I wrestled with that kid for hours, trying to get just one shot of innocence and happiness. It culminated in the kid taking a fire engine and hitting me in the chin, opening my old war wound and blood spurting everywhere."

"What happened?"

"The kid laughed and I snapped the shot. It turned out beautiful and Russ and his wife were thrilled. Trust me, Russ will tell me what we want to know."

Caralie giggled at the mental image of Riley being chased around his studio by a maniacal, fire-engine wielding two-year-old.

"Don't laugh," he commanded, amusement lighting the usual darkness of his eyes. "The kid will probably grow up to be president."

"You like kids?"

"Yeah. I didn't know I did until Kaycee. But in the joys of my fatherhood I discovered the joy of children. What about you? Do you want lots and lots of kids?"

Caralie shrugged. "There was a time when I wanted children...a boy and a girl."

"A dog and a house with a picket fence?"

"Exactly," she said with a nod. "The American Dream. Loretta and I used to talk about those things a lot when we were younger."

"And now?"

She stared down into her tea, as if the residue in the bottom of the cup held all the answers she sought. "David doesn't want biological children." She looked at Riley. "There are so many children in need of good homes already here, he figures it would be better to adopt some of them than to add to the problem of overpopulation."

"Okay, you've told me what David wants." Riley gazed at her intently. "Now tell me what Caralie Tracey wants."

"I want what David wants," she replied, but the words sounded hollow to her ears and left behind a strange, unpleasant taste. She sipped her tea to dispel it.

"I hope Sebastian can tell us something more if we talk to him again tomorrow. Maybe he didn't want to say too much in front of the landlady," Caralie said. She felt safer with the conversation back on Loretta's mystery.

"Maybe—or maybe he's the one who threw the brick through my window," Riley said. "He certainly had the muscle to heft a concrete block over his head and toss it."

Caralie rubbed her forehead. "Everything is so confusing."

"We should probably call it a night. Things are usually clearer in the morning."

Caralie nodded. Unfortunately she had a feeling that the more time she spent with Riley, the less clear things would become.

Chapter Seven

"Okay, I've got the address where the taxi driver dropped our Goldilocks," Riley said as he entered the kitchen where Caralie was in the process of making lunch for the three of them.

They had gotten up early and gone to pick up Kaycee from Riley's mother. For the remainder of the morning, Caralie had played with Kaycee while Riley stayed on the phone, first trying to contact Russ, then attempting to connect with the driver of the cab.

"Where?" Caralie asked as she pulled a hot casserole out of the oven.

Riley watched in fascination as she blew a strand of hair from her face. The heat from the open oven door had pulled pink color into her cheeks. Kaycee sat in her high chair, happily chewing on a cracker. The early-afternoon sunlight played through the window, giving the room a golden glow that added to the warm domesticity of the scene.

Anyone peeking in the window right now would see a family. They wouldn't know that the man and woman were at odds, fighting over the fate of the little girl they both loved.

"Riley?"

He started from his thoughts and stared at her. Why in the hell did she have to be so pretty? He'd tossed and turned the night before with disturbing thoughts of her. He felt as if she were unconsciously seducing him, and his desire for her was building to mammoth proportions.

"Riley?" She laughed self-consciously. "You're staring."

"Sorry." Warmth suffused his face and he smiled at his daughter, giving himself a moment to regain his composure. "The driver dropped Goldilocks off at the corner of Hillsdale Road and Beechnut Avenue. I figured we'd take a ride right after we eat."

Caralie placed the dish on the table. "Sounds like a plan to me." She looked at him hesitantly. "I hope you like tuna casserole."

"It's fine," he assured her. "Although I told you earlier that it isn't necessary for you to cook for me."

"If I wasn't staying here, I'd be paying a hotel bill. Cooking is the least I can do to thank you for your hospitality and your help."

For some reason her words irritated him. In fact, at the moment, everything irritated him. The domestic aura, Caralie's sparkling eyes and luscious lips, even Kaycee's happier-than-usual chattering rankled. And he knew the reason was because the appealing scene threatened him.

"Let's eat and get out of here," he said.

Caralie frowned at the abruptness of his tone, but

said nothing. He filled Kaycee's bowl with the noodle-and-tuna concoction, then scooped a portion onto his own plate. Caralie added a tossed salad and hot rolls to the table, then joined him.

They ate in silence, Riley's irritation growing as he watched her eat. He wondered if she had any idea how sensual she was when eating.

He'd noticed it last night at Chubbie's, and it was apparent again now. As she bit into a roll, a dollop of butter decorated her upper lip. Her tongue slid across her lips, capturing the errant drop and causing Riley's blood pressure to soar.

Dammit. He wanted her. And he had no right. She was practically married to "Saint" David, and Riley certainly had no intention of offering her anything permanent. He'd loved once and lost, and he wasn't about to set himself up for that kind of heartache again.

He could seduce her, ravish her body and play right into her hands. By making love to her and offering no commitment, he'd be living up to his reputation as Wild Man Riley and would possibly lose his daughter in the process.

"Are you having second thoughts about all this?" she asked softly.

"Second thoughts about what?"

She shrugged. "About my being here... About seeking answers to Loretta's death... About all of it."

"Of course not," he scoffed.

"Then why are you angry?"

He set his fork down and looked at her. "Why do you think I'm angry?"

"Because your jaw is pulsing."

Riley lifted a hand to touch the side of his face, where his jaw muscle was taut—and indeed pulsing. "I just have a lot on my mind," he replied.

"Have you had to cancel clients the last couple of days?" she asked, a worried frown producing an endearing wrinkle across her forehead.

"No. I didn't schedule anything between Christmas and New Year's. I wanted a break."

He felt his aggravation ebb as their conversation continued. "The month before Christmas, I was doing three or four sittings a day. Everyone wants holiday photos."

"That must be fun—taking pictures of families dressed in their best finery, capturing a moment of togetherness on film."

Riley smiled. "I always believed that photographing an approaching storm or the aftermath of an earthquake was a challenge." He shook his head ruefully. "I never knew what a real challenge was until I tried to get a family of four or six or eight to all smile at the same time."

"The first day I arrived there was a woman leaving your office with a big, fat dog."

Riley nodded. "That was Sir Henry. He gets his picture taken on every major holiday." He carried his empty plate to the sink and Caralie did the same.

As they cleaned up the kitchen, Riley entertained her with Sir Henry stories. He enjoyed the sound of her laughter, guessed that joy and laughter hadn't been a big part of her life in the past.

When the dishes were done, Riley washed up Kaycee, who wore more of the casserole than she'd eaten. Within thirty minutes they were in Riley's car, headed back to Loretta's apartment building to speak to her neighbor, Sebastian. After talking to him, they intended to check out the area where the cabdriver had dropped off Goldilocks.

Sebastian opened his door at their second knock, his pale blue eyes registering surprise. "Mr. Kincaid and Ms. Tracey, isn't it?"

Riley nodded. "We're sorry to bother you again, Mr. McCullough, but we were wondering if we could ask you a few more questions about Loretta."

Sebastian hesitated, his gaze lingering on Kaycee, then he stepped aside to allow them into his apartment. "Please...have a seat." He gestured them toward an overstuffed navy sofa, then sat in a chair facing them. "Is she Loretta's?" he asked, looking once again at Kaycee.

Riley nodded curtly.

Sebastian nodded. "She looks like her mother." He cleared his throat. "Now, how can I help you?"

"You mentioned that you were fairly friendly with Loretta when we spoke to you before," Caralie said.

"Yes, we were friendly. Loretta often came over here in the evenings when I'd get home from work. She was a very lonely young woman."

Riley saw the spasm of guilt that crossed Caralie's face. "She had no friends? You never saw anyone coming and going from her apartment?" Riley asked.

"And you have no idea what she was doing to earn a living?" Caralie added.

A smile slowly stretched across Sebastian's plain face. "For the first couple of months after Loretta moved in here, I suspected she might be a prostitute."

He smiled in apology to Caralie, who appeared horrified at the very thought. "I quickly realized I was wrong. She had no men coming in and out of her place, didn't seem particularly dependent on the telephone. I confessed my suspicions to her after I got to know her and she howled with laughter." He shook his head, a smile once again stretching his lips at the memory. "She told me she was living off an inheritance and didn't have to work." He shrugged. "I had no reason not to believe her."

Riley studied the man across from him. "You loved her, didn't you?"

Caralie looked at Riley in astonishment, but Sebastian eyed him steadily, seemingly unsurprised by the question. "I did," he admitted. "But it was definitely a case of unrequited love. Loretta saw me as a good friend, a cherished companion, but definitely not a love interest."

"Didn't that upset you?"

Sebastian sighed and averted his gaze from Riley's. "It broke my heart. However, I was willing to accept whatever she had to offer me, and I treasure the time we had to spend together." He looked at Kaycee once again, who was enthralled with Riley's set of keys. "Of course, when Loretta's pregnancy became obvious, I realized she had someone else in her life.''

''But you don't know who it was?'' Caralie pressed.

Sebastian shook his head. ''About once every two weeks, Loretta would leave and be gone all night. She told me she was visiting family, but I guessed she was seeing whoever she was involved with. There were areas in Loretta's life where I didn't pry.''

''And you never saw anyone visiting her?'' Riley felt Caralie's frustration radiating from her as she asked the question.

''Actually, she did have a couple of visitors the week before the fire. A woman came one night and then several nights later two men dropped in to see her. I asked her about them, who they were, and she said something about 'Goldilocks and the two bears.'''

Electric-like energy surged through Riley as his gaze met Caralie's. *Goldilocks.* Who in the hell was she and what, if anything, did she have to do with Loretta's death? ''She didn't elaborate?'' Riley asked.

''No. In fact, I got the impression she was sorry she'd said that much.'' Sebastian held out his hands in a gesture of emptiness. ''I'm afraid that's all I can tell you.''

''We thank you for your time,'' Riley said as he stood and shifted Kaycee to the crook of his arm.

''I'm sorry I couldn't be more help. Loretta and I spent lots of time together, but she had secrets—secrets she wouldn't divulge even to me,'' Sebastian said, as he walked them to the front door.

''Well, I'm even more confused than I was before,'' Caralie said when they were back in the car. She turned in her seat and eyed Riley curiously. ''How did you know he was in love with Loretta?''

''It was just a lucky guess. I don't know.... Maybe it was the way he looked at Kaycee.''

''So we should cross him off our list of suspects?'' she asked.

''No. It's possible we should move him to the top of the list.'' Riley felt Caralie's gaze on him as he started the car. Instead of putting the car into gear, he twisted in his seat to face her. ''Think about it. Sebastian was in love with Loretta and she died on the night she gave birth to another man's child.'' An arrow of guilt pierced him as he recognized his own role in Loretta's life. ''Maybe he loved her so much he snapped that night, became overwhelmed by the fact that his love was unrequited. Maybe he decided if he couldn't have her, nobody else would.''

Caralie frowned. ''That's not love. That's sick obsession. Love is about letting go. If you love someone you let them go where they will be most happy, you don't cling selfishly.''

Riley didn't respond. He put the car in gear and pulled away from the curb. Was that what he was doing with Kaycee? Clinging selfishly? Would she be happier being raised by Caralie?

Certainly he'd lost many hours of sleep in the first month of Kaycee's life. He'd worried about his parenting skills, wondered how he would handle raising a little girl as she got older. But those worries had disappeared amid the daily tasks of looking after Kaycee, evaporated in the simple joy of loving her.

He shoved these thoughts from his head. He knew he was the best choice for raising Kaycee. Nobody could love her as he did—with all his heart, all his soul. And that was all she needed to be healthy and happy.

The address he'd received from Russ took them to an area of South Houston where whole buildings were abandoned and what few businesses remained had iron bars across the windows. Where, crime was rampant but poverty and hopelessness remained the true culprits.

The traffic became sporadic and he felt Caralie's unease growing along with his own. "Not exactly a great area," she murmured as they passed a corner where half-a-dozen gang members loitered, wearing their colors like badges of honor.

"The corner is right up ahead," Riley said as he maneuvered over to the curb in front of a small neighborhood liquor store. "I think it's best if we stay in the car."

"You won't get any arguments from me," Caralie replied dryly. She unbuckled her seat belt and turned around to smile at Kaycee, who babbled happily to the stuffed cat Caralie had bought the previous morning. "So, basically, this is a stakeout," she said as she looked around.

"Yeah," he agreed.

"Do you think maybe Goldilocks lives around here?" she asked.

Riley gazed out the car window, scanning the buildings at the corner—a small grocery store, a health clinic and two apartment buildings. "Either she lives around here or has friends here. I can't imagine any other reason for her to come to this area."

"How many apartments do you think are in those buildings?" Caralie asked.

Once again Riley looked at the brick high-rises that faced each other like ancient sentries guarding the intersection. "I don't know. Maybe four to a floor, and they're about fifteen stories high."

"So, we're talking maybe sixty or more apartments." Her voice held a tinge of hopelessness.

"Nobody said this was going to be easy. We've just got to hope that this is Goldilocks's stomping grounds and that sooner or later she'll make an appearance."

"I wonder why she ran from you last night. I mean, she didn't know us, had no idea why we wanted to talk to her. Why would she just take off?"

The same questions had plagued Riley all night long. Why had she run? Had he called her by the name Goldilocks? He couldn't remember. "Somebody must have warned her that we were asking questions. I can't help but think she has to know something about Loretta and whoever sent those threatening notes to Loretta."

"I know. But who...and why?" Caralie sighed and rippled her fingers through the length of her hair.

For the past several days she'd worn it confined in a braid, but today she'd left it loose. It skimmed her shoulders and flowed down her back, like a dark waterfall sprinkled with moon dust. Riley tightened his hands on the steering wheel, fighting an impulse to reach out and lose his fingers in the dark silk of it.

"Maybe I should go over there and check the names on the mailboxes," he said, feeling the need to get out of the close confines of the car, escape her nearness.

"And do you really think you'll find the name 'Goldilocks' on one of the mailboxes?" she asked.

Riley rubbed his forehead as he realized this had been a bad idea. He should have come alone. He should have insisted Caralie remain behind with Kaycee.

It was ridiculous to try to do a stakeout for any length of time with an eight-month-old baby and a woman whose very presence muddied his senses.

"You're jaw is pulsing again," she observed.

"I'm frustrated. I can't figure out what we've managed to walk into." He dropped his hands from the steering wheel. "My old newspaper buddies used to say I had a nose for danger, and my nose has been itching with the scent of it for the last couple of days."

"Maybe we should just drop it. Maybe we should forget the whole thing." Her tone held no conviction.

He grinned wryly, knowing she'd spoken the words more for his benefit than with any real desire to halt their investigation. "If you read all the articles that have been published about me, then you know I never back away from danger. I usually run right into the middle of it."

"And so far you've managed to get back out of it again, which is why I trust you. And it's why I'm glad you're in this with me."

For a moment their gazes met and held. Again Riley had to remind himself that they were partners for now, with the common goal of getting to the reason for Loretta's death. But when this was all over, they would be opponents in a game with impossibly high stakes.

He broke eye contact with her and looked into the back seat where Kaycee had fallen asleep, the kitty clutched loosely in her arms. "You told me the other day that your mother dropped you off at a shelter when you were six and Loretta was eight. Did your mom ever come back to find you?"

Caralie shook her head. "Not that I'm aware of."

They both looked at one of the apartment buildings where a group of young people had walked out, but the blonde they sought was not among them.

"Mother wasn't a bad woman, she was just weak," Caralie said, picking up the thread of the conversation. "Like Loretta, Mother made bad choices. We lived in dozens of places, always with a different 'Daddy.' When there wasn't a man in her life she drank too much and disappeared for days at a time. I've always believed she did the kindest thing for us in giving us up."

"What about your father?"

"He died in a car accident right after I was born,"

she explained. ''I think that's when Mother went a little crazy.''

Again their attention was drawn to people drifting out of one of the apartment buildings. ''Tell me about your childhood,'' Caralie said a moment later.

For the next hour Riley spoke of his youth, telling one story after another, as Caralie proved to be an avid listener. He found himself recalling amusing incidents to share with her, just to see the way her laughter made her eyes sparkle and deepened their gray hue to dark charcoal.

As he spoke of all those crazy moments in time that make up memories, he realized how much Caralie and Loretta had lost in their youth. They'd had no continuity, no stability—both things he had never thought about, had taken for granted in his own growing-up years.

He suddenly wondered if Caralie wanted custody of Kaycee because she truly believed she would be the better parent, or because she needed Kaycee to somehow recreate and live out all the things she hadn't had in her own childhood. He knew it was probably too big a void for a child to fill, and he wondered if Caralie recognized that.

When he could think of no more stories, no more memories to share, silence grew between them. It wasn't an awkward silence, but rather a comfortable one. He glanced over at her. Her brow was furrowed in apparent deep thought.

''There's one thing that's been bothering me,'' she said finally.

''What's that?''

"Sebastian said that Loretta referred to the two men who came to visit her as 'the two bears.'"

"Yeah, so why does that bother you?" he asked curiously.

"Because the fairy tale is about Goldilocks and the *three* bears. I keep thinking there's a player in all this we haven't met yet, or don't know about."

Riley laughed dryly. "I'd say there's a lot about all this we don't know about." He stretched as much as he could, knew he would be stiff from sitting for so long. His ribs were still sore from the beating he'd received, but the cut on his chin, as usual, was healing quickly.

He looked at his watch. It was almost five. They'd been sitting in the car for nearly three hours. "This was probably a crazy idea," he said ruefully. "I was hoping we'd catch a glimpse of our mystery woman coming or going and pinpoint where she lives."

"It wasn't a crazy idea," Caralie protested. "It isn't like we have a whole bunch of leads to follow."

"I'd like to find the sicko who butchered Kaycee's stuffed animal and broke my plate-glass window." He frowned thoughtfully. "I can't figure out what the connection is between all these people and Loretta." He looked at Caralie. "You don't think it's possible Loretta was involved with drugs in some way?"

"No." The answer came firmly, emphatically. "Loretta was weak, but she wasn't stupid, and she was vehemently against drugs."

"Yeah, and I figure if we were threatening some drug czar's empire with our questions, it would have been a bomb that flew through my window instead of a brick.''

''But we've obviously threatened somebody or something,'' Caralie replied.

''Yeah, and I have a feeling the only way we're going to get answers is to keep asking questions and hope that whoever we're making nervous shows themselves.''

Caralie shivered, as if the chill outside the car had suddenly invaded the warm interior, and Riley fought his desire to take her in his arms and assure her that everything would be all right.

Kaycee woke up, fussier than usual. Caralie instantly turned in her seat and tried to soothe the baby. ''She's probably hungry,'' Riley said, knowing his little girl's hungry sound from her genuine cries of distress. ''We might as well call it a day.'' He turned the key to start the engine. ''I've got an old friend who might be able to help us with all this.''

''Who?'' Caralie asked as she rebuckled her seat belt.

''Stanley Walker. He's an investigative reporter and does a little private investigation on the side. I'll give him our list of suspects, and the description and this address for Goldilocks, and we'll see what he can come up with.''

He pulled away from the curb. ''Stanley has resources I don't have and maybe by doing a thorough background check on these people he can come up with something for us.''

''Sounds like a great idea.'' She smiled at him—a hundred-watt smile that warmed his insides.

Without warning, their car was jolted from behind—a metal-screeching, bone-jarring bump that jerked Riley's head forward, then backward. Caralie screamed and Kaycee let loose a banshee cry of terror as they were hit again, this time with more force.

''What the he—'' Riley swallowed the last of his curse as yet again the back of his car was rammed. There was no way to mistake the actions of the car behind them as accidental or inadvertent.

Fighting the natural impulse to brake, he instead pressed on the gas, grateful for the burst of power that placed distance between his car and the attacking vehicle. If Kaycee and Caralie weren't with him, he'd stop the car and face his opponent. But he couldn't risk Caralie and the baby's safety.

However, his relief was short-lived. Whatever the offensive car had beneath the hood, it was more than Riley's car had.

''Hang on,'' he instructed Caralie, shouting to be heard above the din of Kaycee's cries. With a jerk of the wheel, he careened around a corner.

He was afraid of losing control, but more afraid of stopping the car and facing whoever was in the vehicle behind them. The setting sun reflecting in his rearview mirror made it difficult for him to see not only who was driving the sturdy, high-power model, but also how many people were inside.

Heading for the freeway entrance, Riley once again floored the gas pedal, attempting to put distance between them and their pursuer. On the freeway there would be traffic—witnesses.

He was aware how vulnerable they were, here on

the side streets. There was very little traffic, and he had a feeling that whatever witnesses there might be to a crime would disappear with the arrival of the first police car.

He shot a quick glance at Caralie, noting the utter wash of color from her face and her eyes widened in fear. With her visage frozen in his mind and Kaycee's hysterical cries ringing in his ears, anger welled up inside him.

Damn them. Who were they? What did they want? A glance in the mirror confirmed the car was gaining on them. "Hold on!" he cried just before they were smashed again.

He heard Caralie's hysterical sob as he turned up the ramp that led to the freeway. For the first time in his life he was grateful for the Houston traffic. He eased into the slow lane, his gaze darting to the rear-view mirror.

Where was it?

Where was the car?

His answer came as the aggressor slammed into the driver's side, pushing them toward the guardrail. Riley fought the wheel, struggling to keep the car on the road and away from the rail and the embankment beyond.

He glanced at Caralie, saw her mouth open. He knew she must be screaming, but the sound was lost amid the screech of metal as the cars remained crunched together. Sparks flew as the two continued making contact. Other cars pulled off the pavement or swerved to avoid being hit by the two conjoined vehicles.

Still maneuvering to remain on the road, Riley tried to see into the car, but dark-tinted windows made it impossible to see the occupants.

In a desperate attempt to break free, Riley jammed on the brakes. There was a loud pop and the car careened out of control. As the attacking car continued forward, Riley frantically fought the wheel, knowing he'd blown a tire.

The guardrail ripped away as they barreled through it. He saw the embankment and knew he couldn't stop their descent. Down they went, hurtling over bumps and hollows. Riley rode the brakes, desperately trying to steer the car so they wouldn't flip over.

With a loud crash, their forward motion halted—stopped by the huge wooden post of a billboard sign. Instantly Riley jerked around in his seat to check his daughter. She appeared unharmed, although she sobbed deep, hiccuping cries.

''It's okay, honey,'' he said as he unbuckled his seat belt. ''Caralie...you okay?''

When there was no answer, he turned to look at her. She lay slumped against the broken passenger-side window, blood trekking down the side of her face. Horror washed over him. Was she dead?

''Hey, everyone all right in there?'' a voice called from outside the car.

Riley saw a man running toward them. Clad in a flowered shirt and Bermuda shorts with a camera slung around his neck, the man was obviously a tourist. ''I called the police on my cell phone!'' he yelled.

Riley stepped out of the car, his heart beating a rhythm of panic. "Tell them we need an ambulance!" he shouted back. He looked again at Caralie. She hadn't moved and her face was blanched of color. "And tell them to hurry!" he added, praying that it wasn't already too late.

Chapter Eight

''Honestly, Riley, I'm fine,'' Caralie assured him for the third time as they left the emergency room. ''The doctor said the cut is superficial and I don't have a concussion.''

Riley shifted the sleeping Kaycee from one hip to the other, his face lined with a combination of worry and exhaustion. ''It's a miracle we weren't all killed,'' he said, his voice tight with residual anger and frustration.

It was after midnight and the air was cold, as cold as the chilling winds that blew through Caralie as she remembered those moments of terror on the highway. As she saw Riley's damaged car, the chill intensified.

''Oh, Riley. What a mess!'' she said in dismay. The rear of the car was crunched, the front dented and the driver's side looked as if an attempt had been made to open it like a can of sardines.

''It's mostly cosmetic,'' he replied. ''At least it still runs.''

Caralie felt tears press ominously close as she

gazed at the destruction of his car. She knew the emotion was a result of her aching head and the horrifying car chase they'd been through.

As Riley settled Kaycee in her infant seat in the back, Caralie got into the passenger seat, careful not to disturb the spiderweb of broken glass where her head had cracked against the window.

She'd wanted to learn the truth about her sister's death, but at what cost? The sight of the damage to Riley's car horrified her. The thought that Kaycee had been in the back seat, that she could have been hurt—or worse—terrified her.

They were playing a game with no rules, and the stakes had become far too high. "We have to stop," she said to Riley as he slid in behind the wheel.

He turned and looked at her in bewilderment. "Pardon me?"

"We have to stop, Riley. Stop asking questions, stop stirring up trouble." She wrapped her arms around her shoulders, cold from the inside out. "I don't know what we've managed to get involved in, but we can't continue."

"I didn't have you pegged as a quitter," he replied.

She flushed, surprised to find that his opinion of her mattered. "I'm usually not, and if I were just worried about me, I wouldn't quit—no matter what." She turned and gazed at Kaycee, who smiled sleepily and rubbed her eyes with tiny fists.

"I called my mother from the hospital. She's going to watch Kaycee for a week or two." He started the car, then turned back to Caralie. "You can quit if you like, but I'm not stopping.'' In the glow from the dashboard his features looked hard, dangerous. She knew she was getting a glimpse of the man he had been—Wild Man Riley.

''I won't quit. If you can assure me Kaycee will be safe, then I'm in this until the end.''

''Kaycee will be safe,'' he promised. His features softened and he grinned at her. ''God help anyone who tries to get past my mother. She'd chew them up and spit them out.''

Caralie smiled, the smile instantly transforming into a grimace as the pounding in the side of her head intensified.

''Did they give you anything for the pain?'' he asked, obviously noticing her discomfort.

''No. The last thing I wanted was to be muddy-headed by medication. I'll be fine with a couple of aspirin and a good night's sleep.''

''I'll call Stanley first thing in the morning and get him started on background checks of everyone we know who might be involved. We'll lay low for the next couple of days, lick our wounds and recuperate.''

Caralie leaned her head back against the seat. At the moment, a day or two of rest sounded like a sinful indulgence and was wonderfully welcome. ''How did they know where we were?'' It was a question that had plagued her the entire time she had been in with the doctor. ''How did they know where we were?''

Riley sighed and raked a hand through his hair. ''I don't know. Either we were followed or Goldilocks saw us and told somebody we were there. We could have been followed from my place or from Sebastian's."

The thought that Sebastian or someone else had tailed them, watched as they sat in the car and kept an eye out for Goldilocks, seemed unbelievable. But, the events of the last couple of days seemed equally unbelievable.

Within minutes they were at Riley's mother's house. As Riley got Kaycee out of the back seat, Caralie also got out of the car. Riley seemed to sense her need and held the little girl out to her.

Caralie took Kaycee into her arms. Kaycee grinned and grabbed Caralie's nose. The resilience of children, Caralie thought enviously. Those moments of fear, of terror-filled cries, had apparently been forgotten by the little girl.

For a moment Caralie burrowed her face in the sweet skin of Kaycee's neck, smelling the baby-powder scent of innocence. It broke her heart to think that somehow she'd brought danger to this child; that because of her, Kaycee was being put out of her home. Because of her own obsession and need to uncover the mystery of Loretta's death, Riley's and Kaycee's lives had been completely disrupted.

"It will be all right," he said softly, as if aware of her inner turmoil. Gently he took Kaycee from her. "She loves her grandma and this is only temporary."

Caralie nodded. As he carried Kaycee to the house, Caralie got back in the car. Once again, hot tears pressed at her eyes. *Oh, Loretta, what were you mixed up in?* she thought. *What hole of madness did you fall into?*

It was several minutes before Riley returned to the car, his features strained. "My mother thinks we've both lost our minds," he said.

Without conscious thought, Caralie reached over and placed a hand on his thigh. "I'm sorry. I'm so sorry about all of this."

"You have nothing to be sorry about." His eyes gleamed in the near darkness. "Besides, my mother has always thought I was half crazy. This all simply confirms her suspicions."

Caralie felt the tautness of his leg muscle beneath her palm. She pulled her hand away, far too aware of him. What she wanted to do was curl up in his arms, have him hold her through the darkness of the night.

With a sigh she reached up and touched the tender lump on her head. Apparently she'd managed to scramble her brains when she'd crashed into the window.

"You okay?" he asked, his voice a low rumble.

She nodded. "Just tired."

By the time they got back to Riley's house, her head pounded with nauseating intensity. As they walked through the living room, Riley noticed the red light blinking on his answering machine, indicating messages waiting. He punched the playback button.

"You've been warned twice to mind your own business. Three strikes and you're out." The deep, male voice reverberated through the small living room.

"I guess we now know for sure that what happened tonight wasn't just a random act of violence," Riley said, his voice tight with anger. He looked at Caralie, his features relaxing somewhat. "Go to bed," he said gently. "We'll sort things out in the morning."

Caralie didn't argue with him. Despite the headache, she slept long and deeply. It was after ten when she woke the next morning. After a quick shower, she found Riley sitting at the kitchen table.

"Good morning," he greeted her as he looked up from the paperwork in front of him. "How's your head?"

Caralie touched it gingerly. "Better, I think. At least it isn't hurting at the moment." She poured herself a cup of coffee and sank down across from him at the table.

"I got hold of Stanley a little while ago. He's on his way over. I'm making a list of the people I want him to run background checks on," he explained. "I'm going to tell him to check it all—employment history, financial status, I want to know everything he can find out about these people. Someplace on this list is somebody who either was responsible or knows who is responsible for Loretta's death."

"Can I see the list?"

"Sure." He handed her the sheet of paper.

He'd listed everyone they had spoken to, beginning at the Houston hospital and ending with the mysterious Goldilocks. "You really think Mayor

Monroe has anything to do with this?'' she asked as she spotted his name among the others.

Riley shrugged. ''Who knows? We know the receptionist gave him your message because he called here. He's a link to Loretta.''

''But when I spoke to him I got the impression he didn't even remember Loretta.''

Riley cast her a droll smile. ''He's a politician. He gets paid to lie.''

''You're a cynic,'' Caralie said as she handed the list back to him.

He laughed. ''I prefer to think of myself as a realist.'' His smile faded. ''Maybe Loretta stumbled on illegal campaign funding or kickbacks on city contracts.''

Caralie frowned. ''I find it hard to believe that Loretta would recognize things like that.''

Again Riley shrugged. ''It's just one theory among a hundred. It's also possible Sebastian knows more than he told us...or Tommy at Tommy's Tavern had something against your sister.'' He held out his hands in a gesture of emptiness. ''Speculation—that's all we have.''

A knock on the back door interrupted their conversation. Riley opened the door and was instantly enveloped in a bear hug by a short, squat man with a shining bald pate.

After the initial male ceremony of backslaps and shoulder jabs, Riley introduced Caralie to Stanley Walker, who took her hand and grandly kissed the back of it with a courtly bow. ''We've all been theorizing on what sort of woman could tame the Wild

Man. We knew she'd have to be a knockout, and we were right.''

''Oh, I'm not—I didn't—'' Caralie stuttered and shot a helpless look at Riley.

''Sit down, Stanley, and let me pour you a cup of coffee,'' Riley said, his eyes filled with laughter at Caralie's obvious discomfort over Stanley's mistaken assumption.

''Yes, sir. Riley was one crazy guy when he was working with me,'' Stanley said as he eased himself into a chair at the table. ''There were times when we thought he might be one crayon short of a box.''

''Indeed.'' Caralie smiled at Stanley in encouragement. ''I'd love to hear about those crazy times.''

''It's the past,'' Riley said. ''You don't want to hear about history.'' He looked decidedly uncomfortable with this turn in the conversation.

''Hey, Riley, remember that time in Mexico when those two señoritas chased you with knives?'' Stanley roared with laughter. Riley frowned irritably. ''Did he tell you about that?'' Stanley asked Caralie.

''No, but I'm sure I'd find it fascinating,'' Caralie replied, amused by Riley's slight flush.

''Why don't we get right to the reason you're here,'' Riley countered.

''You mentioned something about murder and mayhem on the phone.'' Stanley grinned. ''You know how words like that whet my appetite.''

As Riley explained to Stanley everything about their situation, starting with Loretta's phone call to him announcing his impending fatherhood and ending with the accident and message of the night before, Caralie found herself studying Riley's face.

Taken feature by feature, there was nothing special or arresting about Riley Kincaid. But somehow when taken all together as a whole, his face radiated not only intelligence, but a primal sexual attractiveness she felt all the way to the pit of her stomach.

She remembered those moments of weakness from the night before, when she'd wished he'd take her in his arms, hold her tight and make her feel safe. Weakness. That was what it had been. She'd watched both her mother and her sister succumb to such weakness, ending up with men all wrong for them in an effort to avoid being alone. She refused to make the same mistake.

Stanley took the list of suspects from Riley and looked it over. "Pretty diverse bunch of people," he observed. "The mayor, a bar owner, a couple of nurses and sundry other citizens."

"And we aren't even sure the guilty party is on that list," Caralie added. "But somebody there definitely knows more than they're telling about my sister's death."

"I'll check them out," Stanley agreed. "Although it might be a day or two before I can get back to you. The holiday tomorrow will hamper my efforts at obtaining information."

Caralie was surprised to realize tomorrow was New Year's Day. That meant tonight was New Year's Eve. A time for renewing old friendships, celebrating the birth of a New Year and looking back without regret. Depression settled over her as she thought of ringing in the New Year without her sister and without answers to what had happened.

She and Riley walked Stanley to the door, where he promised to get back to them as soon as he knew anything.

"I'd forgotten tonight was New Year's Eve," Caralie said when Stanley was gone and she and Riley had returned to the kitchen. "Riley, I don't want to keep you from going out, you know...if you had plans for the evening."

He grinned at her—the devastatingly charming smile that warmed her down to her toes. "My plans had been for Kaycee and me to wear funny hats and toast at midnight with a glass of grape juice. Now I'm hoping I can talk you into the same thing."

"I'll be glad to toast with a glass of grape juice, but I'm afraid I draw the line at wearing a funny hat."

"Rats, I knew you were a conservative at heart," he teased. "How about some breakfast? I make a mean omelet."

"Sounds good," Caralie agreed.

Breakfast was pleasant. As Riley had promised, he made a mean omelet, packed with cheese and mushrooms and fresh vegetables between layers of fluffy cooked eggs. It seemed odd, sitting in the kitchen without Kaycee there. Still, the conversation flowed easily between them.

"Are you going to tell me about the Señoritas in Mexico?" Caralie asked with a teasing grin as they cleaned up after the meal.

Riley looked at her, his dark eyes lit with humor.

''I don't think we know each other well enough for me to share that story with you now.''

''Hmm, you make me more and more curious.''

''Stanley has a big mouth,'' he exclaimed as he handed her the last plate to dry.

She laughed. ''He seems like a nice guy.''

Riley nodded. ''He's one of the best. Stanley and I go way back, and I'd trust him to watch my back in any circumstances.''

Caralie frowned, a niggling ache appearing at the place where she'd banged her head. ''I hope he has us covered in this instance. I have a feeling we need somebody watching our backs.''

Riley's frown mirrored her own. ''I hate to admit it, but I think you're right.''

For a moment their gaze's met and held. Caralie knew that if he looked deep into her eyes he'd see fear and uncertainty, and perhaps the vague whisper of desire. She quickly averted her gaze from his before he could see that particular unwanted emotion.

''If you don't mind, I think maybe I'll lie down and take a nap. My head is hurting a bit.''

''You want some aspirin or something?'' he asked.

''No, I'll be fine.''

Caralie went into her bedroom and stretched out across the bed, unsure if her headache was caused by the jolt she'd received the night before or her wayward thoughts concerning Riley.

She closed her eyes and attempted to summon an image of David's features. A sigh of frustration escaped her as she realized her mind didn't fill with visions of David, but instead conjured up a picture of Riley.

Why was it she was having so much trouble remembering the face of the man she loved? Was it possible she didn't really love David? Her headache intensified at this thought. Was it possible she loved David because he was safe? Because her feelings for him lacked passion, were bereft of desire?

Great passion brought great pain. She'd learned that first from her mother, then from her sister. To love somebody with passion made you vulnerable. Was it possible she was afraid of being vulnerable to abandonment again, and had chosen to marry David not because she loved him, but because she *didn't* love him?

She rolled over on her stomach and clutched a pillow to her chest. Ridiculous. She adored David, and she looked forward to building a life with him—a life of stability and companionship, one that included Kaycee.

Closing her eyes, she envisioned that life and eventually fell into a deep, dreamless sleep. She awoke to the golden glow of dusk painting the room. Looking at her watch, she was surprised to discover it was after six. She'd slept away the entire afternoon.

On the kitchen table she found a note telling her Riley was down in the studio.

She went downstairs, but found the studio empty. "Hello?" she called.

"In here." Riley's voice drifted out of what she knew was the darkroom. "You can come in."

She opened the door and stepped into the small

room that smelled of chemicals. Photos hung from clips on a clothesline that was strung across the width of the space.

"I was just doing a little work," Riley said. He stood at a table, a magnifying glass in one hand and a contact sheet in the other. "Come and look at these." He gestured her over to him.

She moved to stand next to him, instantly able to smell his scent—the fragrant essence of soap and shampoo, of shaving cream and a hint of spicy cologne, and beneath it all, the subtle odor of masculinity she'd come to identify as belonging to Riley alone.

She tried to concentrate on the proof sheet he held toward her, attempted to ignore how close he stood, how utterly his scent enveloped her.

They were pictures of Kaycee—Kaycee laughing, Kaycee sleeping, Kaycee playing. Candid shots of the precious moments in a child's day.

"Oh, Riley, these are wonderful," she exclaimed. She laughed at the photo of Kaycee taking a bath, her head covered in bubbles. "Can you make copies for me?"

She looked at him and her breath caught in her throat. She gazed into his dark eyes, saw the fire of desire lighting them. She recognized the emotion as the same that flowed through her.

He stood too close to her, and she was short of breath, as if he breathed the air meant for her. She took a step backward, wanting—needing—to break the electric connection between them.

Her movement away from him did what she'd

hoped it would. He took the contact sheet from her. "Sure, I'll make you copies," he replied. He set the contact sheet on the table, then looked at her again. "When was the last time you sat for a portrait?"

"High school. My senior year," she told him. "Why?"

"I'm in the mood to take some pictures. How about I take some photos of you, sort of commemorating the New Year?"

"Oh, I don't know...."

"Come on, Caralie. Let me photograph you." This time as he gazed intently at her, his eyes were filled not with desire, but rather with the detachment of a professional. "Did you happen to pack a fancy dress in your suitcase? Something festive?"

"I've got a red sheath," she said, still unsure whether or not she wanted her picture taken. But, Riley's enthusiasm was contagious as he grabbed her hand and pulled her out of the darkroom.

"While you get changed, I'll see what kind of settings I have. We'll do something really nice, but fun." He looked at her expectantly. "Well, what are you waiting for?"

With a laugh of acquiescence, she turned and ran up the stairs. Minutes later, clad in the red silk dress, Caralie stood in the bathroom and freshened her makeup. As she applied lipstick that matched the vivid shade of her dress, she felt as if she were dressing for a date with a lover. The errant thought brought excessive color to her cheeks.

She brushed her hair a dozen strokes, then went downstairs to the studio where Riley had set up a stool in front of a backdrop depicting colorful balloons and confetti.

He turned and gazed at her as she walked in. His eyes widened slightly and he released a low whistle. ''You clean up mighty nice, Ms. Tracey.''

Caralie flushed and ran her hands down her sides. ''It's not very fancy...just a plain old red dress.''

''On the contrary. You look understated, but very elegant.'' He held out his hand to her. ''Come on, let's see if I can capture that quality on film.''

She slipped her hand into his and allowed him to lead her across the floor. She perched atop the stool, feeling awkward and silly as Riley turned on the surrounding bright floodlights, then snapped instructions to her.

''Tilt your head slightly to the left...relax your hands in your lap.'' He backed up, grabbed his camera and focused on her. ''Lower your left shoulder...raise your chin.''

Caralie laughed at his rapid fire commands. ''I feel like a contortionist,'' she exclaimed, her pose stiff and unnatural.

He lowered the camera and grinned. ''Sorry.'' His smile fell away. ''This isn't working. I don't like the pose.'' He set the camera down and crossed to where she sat.

''Swing your legs to this side.'' With the same professional detachment she'd noticed before, he efficiently arranged the skirt of her dress around her legs. He took her by the shoulders and turned her upper body slightly, then picked up a strand of her hair and smoothed it over the front of her bodice.

Heat suffused her, and she didn't know if the warmth came from him or from the floodlights. He cupped her chin and tilted her head to one side, his touch achingly gentle and intensifying the evocative heat inside her.

"There," he said, his voice huskier than usual. "That's perfect." He backed away and once again picked up his camera. The camera clicked and whirred as he moved in front of her, telling her where to look, when to smile. "Now laugh," he demanded.

"I can't laugh on command," she protested, then did so at the absurdity of the request.

"Good...that's good! You've got a wonderful laugh."

He took the entire roll. "Relax while I change the film," he said.

Caralie stood and watched as he pulled out the used roll and inserted a new one. "Don't you think you took enough?" she asked.

"Enough stills, but now I'd like to try some action shots." He finished loading the film and moved the stool to the side of the backdrop. "I've had a couple of models contact me about doing portfolio pictures for them. I need the practice in taking movement photos."

"I would think you'd have all the experience you need in taking action shots," Caralie replied.

"Taking pictures of natural disasters and the aftermath of war is quite different than taking photos of beautiful women in motion." He turned on a transistor radio and tuned in to a station playing old rock and roll, then led Caralie in front of the backdrop again. "Dance for me, Caralie," he said as he focused the camera on her.

She shifted from foot to foot, self-conscious and embarrassed. "I can't," she protested. "Riley, I'm not a model. I don't know how to move for pictures."

He dropped the camera from his eyes and smiled. "Forget the camera, forget me. You're a beautiful woman at a New Year's Eve party and the music is playing and you feel that music inside you, a throbbing rhythm that makes it impossible for you to stand still." His voice was low, smooth...almost hypnotic.

Beneath his gaze, with his dark eyes glittering like black diamonds, Caralie began to feel the music pulse its rhythm in the pit of her stomach. She swayed and closed her eyes, allowing the music to fill her and sweep away any remaining self-consciousness.

She moved her hips and feet to the beat of the radio as Riley snapped picture after picture. He paused between shots only to whisper words of encouragement.

At some point, Caralie realized it wasn't the beat of the music that throbbed through her veins, but rather the pulse of desire. Rich and thick, hot and sweet...it permeated her.

The fast-paced song ended and a new tune filled the studio—a soft, slow strain with words that told of lost love and empty lives. Caralie stopped moving and stood still as Riley set his camera down and approached her.

Without hesitation he took her in his arms, as if

the song that was playing was their own and they had danced together to it a thousand times before.

He allowed no space between their bodies, and hers molded to his in a perfect fit. She closed her eyes and let her fingers splay across the expanse of his broad back. Her face found the hollow of his neck and she rubbed her cheek against the smooth, sexy, scented skin.

She was intensely aware of the press of her breasts against his chest, his thighs intimately close to hers, and the undeniable evidence of his surging desire.

Someplace in the back of her mind she knew she should step back, gain some distance, reclaim rationality. But she didn't want to distance herself from him in any way. She wanted to lose herself in him.

His hands caressed her spine, gliding tantalizingly across the center, then dipping low to the top of her buttocks. She felt her heartbeat mirroring Riley's in quickened pace, speaking of the passion that flared between them like a flash fire out of control.

She tilted her head and looked at Riley. He gazed back at her, his eyes lit with the same desire that pulsed in her veins. He lowered his head and captured her lips with his. Tentatively at first, his mouth played over hers. He deepened the kiss, his tongue touching first the tip of hers, then swirling deeper, more intimately.

He stilled his feet. All pretense of dancing halted as the kiss continued—sweet, hot, deep. His lips possessed her completely and she returned the kiss with a growing fervor.

"Caralie," he whispered when finally his mouth left hers. "God help me, but I want you."

She stared at him, dimly realized that now was the time to stop the madness, now was the time to remind him of all the reasons this was wrong. But words of sanity wouldn't come. As she gazed into his eyes, saw the desire there, she knew that for tonight she was a lost soul—lost to madness, lost to the sweet heat of him.

"God help me, Riley. I want you, too," she replied.

Chapter Nine

Neither Riley nor Caralie said a word as Riley took her by the hand and led her up the stairs and into his bedroom, where a lamp on the nightstand created a warm glow.

There was no hesitation in Caralie, no last lingering doubt to disturb her feeling of utter rightness about this moment.

For this moment, she wanted only to be Riley's lover. Tomorrow she could go back to being his partner in the investigation of Loretta's death. Tomorrow she would return to being his adversary, as they fought for what they each believed was best for Kaycee.

Tonight... Just lovers... Just for one single night....

His room was larger than hers. A navy comforter covered the king-size bed and the top of the double dresser was littered with pocket change, bottles of cologne and a book on parenting.

The room smelled of him, that indefinable masculine scent mingling with the fragrance of cologne that belonged to him alone.

The moment they were in the room, he turned off the lamp and plunged them into a darkness broken only by the glow of the streetlights that danced through the windows.

He sat on the edge of the bed and gently pulled her to stand between his thighs. For a long moment his gaze held hers—hungry, yearning.... He seemed to reach inside her and stroke her heart, causing it to pound with frantic anticipation.

Turning her around, he then moved his fingers to the zipper at the top of her dress. Caralie aided his efforts by sweeping her length of hair to one side.

Her breath caught in her throat as the zipper hissed slowly down and his mouth touched each and every inch of skin that was exposed.

Never in her life had she felt such all-consuming need. Never had she been so utterly possessed by desire.

When he'd completely unzipped the dress, she turned back to face him. At the shrug of her shoulders, the dress fell into a scarlet pool at her feet, leaving her clad in her bra, panty hose and wispy underpanties.

Leaning forward, she cupped his face in her palms and kissed him. With a deep groan, he wrapped his arms around her waist and pulled her onto the bed. Their lips met in a fiery explosion of need.

Caralie fumbled with the buttons of his shirt, wanting to feel his bare skin against her own. Still in the midst of the kiss, she managed to unfasten the last button on his shirt. He tore it off, as if he, too, yearned to be flesh to flesh.

A deep moan of pleasure escaped Caralie as he unsnapped her bra and kissed first one breast, then the other. His tongue teased her turgid nipples as she tangled her fingers in his hair, silently urging him not to stop.

However, he did stop. She groaned in protest as he rolled away from her and stood. Then she realized he wasn't withdrawing from her, but had gotten up to remove his slacks. As he did so, Caralie took off her panty hose and kicked them to the end of the bed.

For a moment he hesitated before rejoining her and she knew he was giving her one last chance to halt everything, one final instant to reclaim sanity.

Did she want to stop this right now? Slip off the bed, grab her clothing and run to her own room? She gave herself a moment to think, then held out her arms to him, refusing to consider the alternative of getting up and walking away from him.

Desire had been building between them for the past several days, reaching a fever pitch that neither of them could deny. She could no more stop this from happening than she could stop the sweeping hands of time that would herald the New Year.

When he rejoined her they became all heat and tangled limbs, eager kisses and fevered caresses. "You are so beautiful," he whispered huskily as he drew her panties slowly down her legs. And she saw her reflection in the dark depths of his eyes.

Caralie shivered, aching with the need for him to

fill her, possess her. She'd never before felt such wanton desire, such intense longing to be joined intimately with a man.

His mouth moved everywhere, touching, tasting and filling her with a velvet heat. She reciprocated, wanting to bring him as much pleasure as he brought her.

He whispered words of passion to her, words both sweet and bold, and each and every one stoked higher, hotter the fires that burned inside her.

When she could stand no more, when she feared she might explode if he didn't take her that instant, she gripped him by the shoulders and arched up beneath him.

He responded and entered her in a slow, smooth stroke. For a moment he didn't move and neither did she, as if the sensation of being so completely joined had caused them both to freeze in splendor.

She looked up at him, saw the dark wildness in his eyes—a wildness that gentled as he gazed down at her.

With one hand he caressed her cheek, and the unexpectedness of it was as sensual as anything he'd done so far. That single touch broke the inertia that had momentarily gripped her.

Their hips moved in unison, finding the mirrored rhythm of giving and receiving, pleasuring and being pleasured. Slowly...sweetly...building in intensity and quickening in matching tempo, they moved like lovers long accustomed to each other.

She cried out as she reached her peak and felt her muscles constricting around him. Before she could descend back to earth, he stiffened against her, groaning her name, and again she soared.

Moments later they lay side by side, spent and waiting for their rapid breathing to return to normal.

After long minutes of silence, Riley propped himself on his elbow and looked at her.

"Regrets?"

"A little late for those, isn't it?" she countered.

He smiled and reached out to smooth a strand of her hair away from her face. "Just making sure, that's all. I wouldn't want you to regret this." He rolled over onto his back and crossed his arms beneath his head, his gaze on the ceiling where patterns of light played. "But, it seems like New Year's Eve is the time to think of all the regrets from the past year, and make magnificent plans for the New Year."

Caralie turned onto her side to face him. She pulled the sheet around herself, self-conscious in her nakedness. "You don't strike me as a man who would entertain such thoughts."

"What? You mean planning for a new year?"

She shook her head. "No. You don't seem like the kind who would entertain regrets."

He shrugged. "I don't beat myself up over them, but sure, there are things I'm sorry about."

"Like what?" she asked. This was a side of Riley she hadn't seen before—a softer, more vulnerable aspect.

Once again he turned so they were face-to-face—lovers sharing secrets in the darkness of the night. "I'm sorry that for years I made fun of guys who took pictures of families—guys who were making a living just like I am now.'' He smiled in self-deprecation. ''I never realized how much joy could be found in living a normal life, without walking on the edge of danger.'' His smile deepened. ''Now, your turn.''

She frowned thoughtfully. She had so many regrets she didn't even know where to begin. ''I'm sorry I went to Africa and left Loretta here all alone. I should have been here to take care of her. I feel as if somehow I'm to blame for whatever trouble she got herself into.''

''How long do you think it would have taken for Loretta to be able to take care of herself? By the time she was thirty? Forty?'' he chided gently. ''How many years would you have sacrificed of your own life to raise a sister who was older than you to begin with?''

Again he touched her cheek, this time sweeping the back of his knuckles against her skin in a soft caress. ''Loretta was a grown-up, Caralie. You can't be responsible for her mistakes and you mustn't blame yourself for any trouble she found.''

Tears blurred Caralie's vision. She closed her eyes, willing them away, but to no avail. She hadn't realized until this moment how badly she had needed somebody to say those words that absolved her from responsibility and guilt.

''I spent years cleaning up Loretta's messes. Unpaid bills, obsessed lovers and their angry wives... She didn't seem to understand the havoc her lifestyle and irresponsible choices wreaked on those around her.'' She sighed tremulously. ''And I imagine if I'd been here with her, she still would have found trouble.'' As she said these words, a catch that had ached in her heart released. This time it was she who reached out and touched Riley's cheek—and felt the sensual roughness of a five o'clock shadow. ''Thank you.''

They both jumped as whistles blew and firecrackers exploded and the sound of cheering filled the street. Riley looked at his watch, then smiled at her. ''Happy New Year,'' he said.

''Happy New Year to you, too,'' she replied.

He leaned forward to kiss her and in his eyes she saw the same flames of desire that had so stirred her before. And she knew he intended to make love to her again. She wanted that—wanted him one last time.

The shrill ring of the telephone broke the spell of the moment. ''Must be an old cohort calling to wish me a Happy New Year,'' Riley said. He rolled over and punched the speaker button on the phone next to his bed. ''Hello?''

''Riley? How's your mother?'' The deep, malevolent male voice shot a shiver of apprehension up Caralie's spine. ''I hope she and that little girl are having a safe holiday.'' There was an audible click, then the blare of a dial tone.

Riley shot up to a sitting position and switched on the lamp. As he dialed the phone, Caralie grabbed his arm, knowing the fear that had to be racing inside him; knew because it raced in her.

''Mom,'' he said, the relief audible in his voice.

"I just called to wish you a Happy New Year. Yes, I know what time it is. Everything all right there?" He listened for a moment and nodded to Caralie, letting her know everything seemed to be okay. "Mom, I know this is going to sound crazy, but I want you to pack a couple of bags and catch a flight to Aunt Virginia's place. No, I haven't been drinking. Please, Mom, just do it. Pack bags for you and for Kaycee. I'll call you back in a few minutes and tell you what flight to catch."

"They were okay?" Caralie asked when he'd hung up.

"Yeah. Somebody just wanted to scare me…and they succeeded." He picked up the phone once again. "My Aunt Virginia lives in Kansas City. I'm getting Mom and Kaycee on the first plane out of here. I'll feel better if they're not in town, at least until we know what in the hell we've stirred up."

As he stayed on the phone and made the necessary arrangements, Caralie remained next to him. What had they gotten themselves into? What kind of monsters had they awakened? People who threatened mothers and babies?

It was after two when Stanley called from the airport. Riley had phoned Stanley and asked him to see his mother and his daughter to the airport. He'd instructed Stanley to watch for tails and make certain they had safely boarded the plane.

Only when they knew Riley's mother and Kaycee were safe, did Riley and Caralie fall into an exhausted sleep.

Hours later, Caralie awakened to the late-morning

sun drifting through the window. She vaguely remembered a five o'clock phone call from Riley's mother, telling Riley they had arrived at his aunt's in Kansas City and all was well.

But, of course, all wasn't well. Their questions had stirred up more trouble, more danger than Caralie had ever imagined possible. And their lovemaking had stirred more confusion than she'd ever felt.

For a long moment she remained still, breathing in the scent of Riley that permeated the sheets that covered her and remembering their night of passion.

Her body ached this morning, but it was an ache of fulfillment like none she'd ever known.

She turned over, wanting to see him as he slept, but found herself alone in the bed. She reached out and placed her hand on his pillow, where the imprint of his head remained.

Burrowing beneath the covers, she shivered. Wild Man Riley, who had made her feel more alive than she'd ever felt before. Wild Man Riley, who had stroked her with a gentleness, kissed her with a tenderness she wouldn't have guessed he possessed.

He confused her. He'd managed to eliminate her guilt over Loretta with a few rational words. He was so unlike the jet-setting, danger-seeking man she'd read about.

Was the sensitive, gentle man an act?

A facade to lull her into forgetting the custody issue?

She sat up, irritated by her perplexing thoughts. She couldn't back down on the custody issue. She wanted—needed—Kaycee in her life. It was what

Loretta had wanted. Caralie had to make sure Riley understood that the issues between them remained; they had slept together, but nothing else had changed.

Moments later, as she stood beneath a hot shower, she realized something *had* changed. Something profound. Since making love to Riley, she knew that there was no way she could ever marry David.

All her dreams of marriage and security had exploded beneath the passion Riley had made her feel. He'd made her understand that she would never really be happy with David—who inspired great respect, but no passion. A marriage between them wouldn't be fair to her, but more than that, it wouldn't be fair to David.

And she thought she just might hate Riley Kincaid for having shattered the vision of her future and offered her nothing to take its place.

RILEY STIRRED THE POT of soup he had simmering on the stovetop, his thoughts on the woman he'd left in his bed an hour earlier. He'd heard the shower minutes before, knew it wouldn't be long before she joined him in the kitchen. He tried to anticipate what her reaction would be to their lovemaking the night before.

In the light of dawn, acceptance often turned to regret and he wondered if she'd be angry with herself…with him. He hoped not. He wasn't sorry about what had happened. How could he be? It had been wonderful. Caralie had surprised him, showing him a passionate dimension he'd only guessed she might possess.

"Something smells good."

He turned and looked at her. Clad in a pair of jeans and an oversize T-shirt, she looked calm and collected. He smiled. "Bean soup with lots of black-eyed peas. You know you have to eat black-eyed peas for luck in the New Year."

She wrinkled her nose as she walked over to the coffeemaker. "I think they're gross."

He laughed. "They are, but this is my super-duper soup recipe and mixed up with all the other ingredients, they go down fairly painlessly."

She poured herself a cup of coffee, then leaned against the counter. "I suppose we can use all the luck we can get, so I'd better eat as many of those things as possible." She sipped her coffee. "Any more word from your mother?"

"No. I told her not to call here again, and I don't intend to call her from here. Stanley assured me he wasn't followed to the airport and I can't imagine how anyone could figure out where my mother has gone. She and Kaycee are safe and that's all I need to know for now."

Caralie nodded, her eyes dark and solemn. "Riley...about last night..." She frowned.

"It's all right," he replied. "I forgive you for taking advantage of me."

She blinked once, twice, then laughed and the tension that had followed her into the room dissipated. "You're some piece of work, Riley." She slipped into a chair at the table.

''That's what they tell me,'' he returned lightly. He set his spoon down and poured himself another cup of coffee.

''But seriously,'' she continued. ''You need to know that last night didn't change anything. I still intend to fight you for custody of Kaycee. I still think it would be best that I am the one to raise her.''

He nodded, although as always the very discussion, the very possibility of losing Kaycee caused his heart to constrict painfully. ''I didn't sleep with you in an effort to get you to change your mind.''

She sipped her coffee, as if satisfied she'd made her point. When she lowered her cup, a teasing smile curled the corners of her mouth. ''Now do we know each other well enough for you to tell me the story of the two señoritas?''

He laughed. ''It really isn't that interesting. We'd been down there for two weeks waiting for a volcano to erupt. We camped in a tent without amenities of any kind and by the time the two weeks were over and there had been no eruption, we were all going a little stir-crazy.''

He paused to take a drink of his coffee, then continued. ''Stanley and I decided to pack it in and we headed for the nearest town, where we drowned our frustration in too many tequilas in a little cantina. As my good sense fled, I started flirting a bit with a woman at the end of the bar. I also started flirting a bit with a woman standing near the jukebox.'' He grinned, shamefaced. ''I didn't realize they were sisters, and before long they'd pulled knives on each other, screaming and yelling and calling each other man-stealers. Before any real damage could be done to one another, they realized they should be directing their ire at me.''

He laughed at the memory and shook his head wryly. ''They chased me around that little town twice, both of them threatening to cut off various parts of my body. I remember that as I ran I could hear Stanley shouting, and to this day I'm not sure if he was urging me to run faster or cheering them on to catch me.''

Caralie laughed—as he knew she would—and he allowed the pleasure of her melodic laughter to wash over him. ''You're bad!'' she exclaimed.

''That was a different man than the one you see now.'' He wanted to explain to her that at that time he'd felt he had nothing to live for; nothing except his work to fill his life. He'd existed in a void with a pain in his heart that nothing could assuage. Then Kaycee had arrived and everything had changed.

''Riley, would you do me a favor?'' she asked before he could say all the things that were in his heart.

''Depends. Does it require personal sacrifice or great physical pain?''

She laughed and again delight swooped through him. ''No, nothing like that.'' She sobered, her eyes darkening slightly. ''Would you take me to where Loretta is buried? I...I need to say goodbye.''

''Of course,'' he agreed instantly. ''We'll go right after lunch.'' Besides, he realized there was somebody he needed to finally say goodbye to, as well.

It was after lunch that they took off for the cemetery. As Riley drove, Caralie entertained him with stories of the people in the villages where she'd been, surprising him with her gift for mimicry as she did imitations of some of the bureaucrats her organization had had to deal with.

They both fell silent as he turned the car onto the narrow road that led into the White Chapel Cemetery. They passed the tiny church that had given the place its name and drove on toward the rear of the area.

"I don't think I ever thanked you for seeing to the arrangements for Loretta," Caralie said, her voice heavy with sadness.

"No thanks are necessary. As the mother of my child she belongs here, in the Kincaid-family section. My grandparents once owned this land," he said. "When they sold it to the people who wanted it for a cemetery, part of the deal was that we would retain a large area for our family plots. Although it sounds rather morbid, I think my grandparents liked the idea of generations of Kincaids all resting here together."

"It doesn't sound morbid," Caralie said. "It sounds loving. One generation providing for the others to come."

Riley parked the car in the small graveled area provided.

"It's beautiful here," she said as they walked along one of the pebbled paths. The grounds were perfectly manicured, the decorative bushes and plants neatly trimmed and tended.

"The caretaker does a good job. I've never been

out here when the place didn't look freshly mowed and weeded."

"You come here often?" She eyed him curiously.

"Occasionally." In truth, it had been a while since he'd been here and that surprised him.

There had been a time when he'd come out as often as possible, visiting one particular grave and cursing fate with a vengeance. It was with surprise that he realized the overwhelming, crippling anger and grief that had once accompanied him was now gone, leaving behind only a sobering acceptance.

"There..." He pointed ahead to a shady area where a dozen matching markers rose from the earth. "The Kincaids."

Caralie's footsteps slowed, as if she wasn't sure she was ready to say goodbye to the sister she'd lost. Riley touched her arm lightly. "Are you okay?"

She stopped and turned to face him, her eyes tumultuous gray skies ready to spill rain. "Goodbyes have always been so difficult." A single tear trekked down her cheek.

Riley caught it on his fingertip. "Your sister left a legacy of love behind in Kaycee. Loretta's memory will be with you every day of your life, every moment in your heart."

Caralie straightened her shoulders and Riley wondered how many times in her life she'd had to be strong while watching people leave her life.

As she walked forward, Riley remained behind. She needed time alone to say her goodbyes, time to mourn in private. He watched her, saw that the determination that had stiffened her shoulders only moments before had once again fled. She looked small and vulnerable.

She stopped before she got to the headstone marking her sister's final resting place. She whirled around to face him, her features not twisted in grief as he'd expected, but frozen with fear. ''Riley!'' she screamed.

Heart pounding, he ran toward her. He halted next to her, his gaze riveted on the headstones in front of them. Across the front of Loretta's, somebody had crossed out the first name and written CARALIE in big, bold letters. On the grave next to Loretta's, his own name was written on the headstone. A shiver worked up his spine as he stared at his name and Caralie's. They appeared to have been written as if to portend some dire future.

Chapter Ten

Caralie sank to her knees, unable to stand as she stared at the defaced headstones. Her name. Riley's name. A sick warning from somebody with a sick, evil mind.

Riley appeared frozen as he, too, stared at the defilement. Caralie closed her eyes against the press of hot tears, but they oozed down her cheeks.

What kind of people were they up against? She'd come here prepared to grieve the sister she'd lost, but that grief was momentarily lost to the horror of seeing her own name on a headstone.

"It's chalk."

"What?" She opened her eyes to see Riley swiping at her name with his handkerchief.

"They used some sort of colored chalk. It's coming right off." He cleaned off Loretta's stone, then wiped the letters of his name from the marker beside Loretta's. As he worked, Caralie saw his gaze darting around the area, as if he were checking to see if the perpetrator might be nearby.

Caralie also looked around, her heart still pounding fiercely in her chest. No other cars were parked anywhere in sight. There was no hint of another person lurking in the area.

Riley finished cleaning off the headstone, then walked over to where Caralie knelt in the grass. He held out his hand to help her up, then instantly pulled her against his chest.

She stood rigid for a moment, not wanting to be weak, not wanting to find solace in any man's arms. However, as he enfolded her close, she burrowed against his broad chest and realized that being in his arms didn't feel like weakness; it felt right.

As he continued to hold her, the horror that had initially chilled her when she'd seen her name on the headstone slowly ebbed. In its place the natural grief she'd arrived with at the cemetery returned, and with it came her tears.

"It's all right," Riley murmured as a sob escaped from her. "It was just a stupid terrorist-like attempt to scare us."

She nodded and cried harder. The stress and fear of the past couple of days, along with the grief over losing her sister, were suddenly too much for her to keep inside. She clung to Riley and he held her tight, as if he knew the emotions that roiled through her.

He didn't try to stop her tears. Instead he rubbed her back, allowed her to vent all the emotion that was inside. "Let it go," he murmured into her hair. "That's it. Just let it all go."

She cried until there were no more tears left and the front of Riley's shirt was soaked with her grief. Only then did she finally move out of his embrace.

"Better?" he asked.

"A little." She laughed self-consciously. "I guess that had been building up for a while. It was either cry or explode."

His eyes lit with a teasing light. "I don't recommend exploding. It's just so messy."

She smiled and gestured to the front of his shirt. "Tears can get pretty messy, as well."

"I'll dry."

Taking a deep breath, she walked toward Loretta's grave and knelt by the side. As she stared at her sister's name, visions of Loretta filled her head. She remembered the day their mother had dropped them off at the shelter.

"She'll be back, won't she?" Loretta had asked as she'd clung to Caralie.

"No," Caralie had replied, at six already possessing a grown-up knowledge of their mother's weaknesses. "No, she won't be back. But it's all right. We'll always have each other."

And they had. Until now. A fresh wave of tears seeped from Caralie's eyes as the ache of loss radiated in her heart. *Oh, Loretta, I'll miss you so much,* Caralie's heart cried. It was one thing to have miles separating them, quite another to have death—the final separation.

Caralie reached out and touched the name etched in the stone, silently telling the sister she'd loved a final goodbye.

Loretta had been loving and gentle, but wounded so deeply from a lifetime of disappointment and abandonment. She'd been so vulnerable, and Caralie knew it was her vulnerability that had caused her death.

Someone had taken advantage of Loretta—someone evil. Caralie swiped her tears with the back of her hand and stood, the ache of loss hardening into a ball of anger.

We'll find them, she vowed. *We'll find who was responsible and see that they are punished.* The need for justice burned in the back of her throat, filled her heart with a scalding need.

She turned to find Riley and was surprised to see him kneeling at a grave in an area next to his family's plots. His head was bowed and his eyes were closed as if he were in prayer. Caralie moved closer so she could read the name on the headstone: Angela Burwell.

Riley opened his eyes, as if he sensed Caralie's nearness. He rose to his feet and backed away from the grave.

"Who was she?" Caralie asked, hoping she wasn't intruding.

His gaze didn't meet Caralie's. "Somebody I loved once...years ago... in another lifetime."

His voice held no heavy grief, just a sadness for somebody who had been gone a long time.

Caralie looked again at the headstone. "She was very young when she died."

He nodded. "Only twenty-one." He looked at Caralie, his eyes dark with emotion. "I'd asked her to marry me on the night she was killed. I'd given her a ring, she'd accepted and her family and mine celebrated at a fancy restaurant."

He drew a deep breath, as if continuing was difficult. "I took her home after the celebration and we planned to meet for breakfast the next morning. Apparently sometime that night one of her friends called. The friend had been out of town on a vacation and didn't know about our engagement. Angela decided to meet the girl." He smiled faintly. "She was eager to show off her ring." The smile faded. "Her car was hit by a drunk driver before she ever got to her friend's apartment. Angela was killed instantly."

"Oh, Riley, I'm so sorry." Caralie's heart ached with his loss. Unsure how to comfort him, she reached out and took his hand.

His fingers entwined with hers as his gaze once again returned to the grave. "I went a little crazy when Angela died. I was so hurt…so angry."

"And that's when Wild Man Riley was born," Caralie guessed.

He squeezed her hand. "Yeah, I guess it was. For a year or two I didn't care much whether I lived or died. It was easy to take chances in my work because I just didn't care. It was as if on the day we buried Angela, my soul was buried, too."

And then Kaycee had appeared and given him back his soul. Loretta's child had given his life new meaning, given him a reason to live.

She unclasped his hand, trying to shove away the unwanted conflicting thoughts. She couldn't think of him and his needs. She had to focus on what was best for Kaycee, and she believed in her heart that Kaycee's interests were best served with her.

"Let's get out of here," he said.

"Whoever wrote our names...how did they know we'd come here?" she asked as they started walking back toward the car.

"It wasn't difficult to figure out," he said. "It's logical to assume that you'd want to visit Loretta's grave."

"But how did they know we'd come today?" she asked, needing to make sense of it all.

"They probably didn't. We haven't had any rain in the last couple of days. They could have written our names there a day or two ago."

Caralie wrapped her arms around her shoulders, a chill racing up her spine as she remembered the shock of seeing her own name scribbled across the pale stone. "It's so gruesome."

"Yeah, it was. Gruesome and calculated." He grabbed her hand, as if silently attempting to allay her fears. "It was nothing more than a scare tactic by cowards."

"It wasn't cowards who forced your car off the road," Caralie reminded.

Riley didn't answer, but his hand tightened around hers. "It's not over yet. Hopefully Stanley will be able to come up with something substantial to help us figure out what we're up against."

"And if he doesn't?" Her question hung in the still air.

Riley had no answer.

The drive back to his house was accomplished in silence. Caralie suspected Riley's thoughts were of the young woman he had loved and lost, and she didn't want to intrude on those thoughts.

She tried to imagine what he'd been like as a young man in love. Had he looked at Angela with the same passion-sparked eyes with which he'd gazed at Caralie?

She scowled and stared out the passenger-side window, irritated with herself for entertaining that particular thought. Of course he hadn't looked at Angela the way he'd gazed at her. He'd been in love with Angela; he'd simply wanted Caralie.

Still, the knowledge of his loss of his beloved explained the way he'd lived his life before Kaycee. It explained the obsession with danger, the fast living and the wild dating.

She suspected that Riley, like Loretta, had learned to deal with his pain by never spending a moment alone or in reflection. Great passion led to great pain. Again, that lesson was pounded home.

Loretta had adored their mother, and her abandonment had forever scarred Loretta. Riley had apparently loved his Angela deeply, and losing her had turned his world upside down.

It was easier not to love, not to risk that kind of pain, Caralie thought. That was why she had gravitated toward David, who was a nice companion but a man she could never really love. David had been safe.

"You okay?" Riley asked.

"Fine...why?"

"You're so quiet. I don't want to intrude into your grief but I want to make sure you're okay."

She smiled at him. "I'm quiet because I don't want to intrude on *your* grief."

He blinked in surprise, then shook his head. "I spent my grief over Angela a long time ago. Although it sounds trite, time really does ease the heartache."

Caralie clutched a hand over her heart. "Even though I know that's true, at the moment it seems like an entire lifetime won't be long enough to ease my heartache."

Riley reached across the seat and covered her hand with his. He said nothing. He didn't have to. His touch conveyed a wealth of sensitivity and compassion.

It was at that moment she realized that Riley Kincaid was definitely unsafe. She already knew the heady intensity of his kisses, had experienced his brand of fiery passion. Add to that his compassion and caring, and he was a definite threat to her. If she wasn't careful—if she wasn't strong—she could fall in love with him.

And that would be as dangerous to her well-being as the nameless, faceless men who threatened them.

"SO, WHAT HAVE YOU GOT for us?" Riley asked Stanley impatiently as his old friend sank onto the sofa next to Caralie.

Three days had passed since they'd last spoken with Stanley. Three days of Riley and Caralie trying to stay out of each other's way. Riley had spent most of his time in his studio and Caralie had whiled away the hours holed up in her bedroom.

Riley wondered if she was homesick for David, and for some reason the idea that she might be love-sick irritated him. He looked at his friend eagerly, hoping Stanley had brought them news that would point to a course of action—anything that would break the tension that had been building inside Riley during the past few days of inaction.

''An interesting bunch of characters you gave me to check out,'' Stanley said as he leaned forward and flipped open the briefcase he'd carried in with him. ''And as with most people, they all have secrets they don't want disturbed.'' He smiled like a Cheshire cat.

''Secrets? Such as what?'' Caralie leaned forward, her eyes sparkling with anticipation. Riley frowned. She was so damned beautiful and the tension that he'd felt for the past several days increased. He wanted her again. He wanted her honeyed kisses, her sweet sighs, her husky cries of passion.

He cleared his throat and glared at Stanley. ''Quit being so damned enigmatic and tell us what you've got.''

Stanley pulled a sheaf of papers from the briefcase and spread them out on the coffee table. ''Let's start with the easy ones. The nurses, Edith Webster and Louise Nelson. Nothing much there. Edith is married and has two grown children. She's the doting grandmother of five grandchildren. Finances seem okay, although they have a lot of credit-card debt. I'd say you can cross Edith Webster off your list of suspects.''

''What about Louise Nelson?'' Riley asked.

''Divorced, constantly struggling to make ends meet. She often works double shifts and seems to have little life outside her work. I'd say she can get a red line through her name, as well.'' Stanley set those papers aside and grinned at the two of them.

Riley gritted his teeth as the reporter played the moment of drama to the hilt. ''Would you get on with it, Stanley.''

Stanley smiled at Caralie. ''I guess you've noticed by now that Riley's strong suit isn't patience.''

''On the contrary, you should see him with his daughter.''

Riley's heart warmed at her unexpected praise. Was it possible she was starting to see things his way? Realize that he was the right one, the only one to raise Kaycee?

''Now is where it gets interesting,'' Stanley said, pulling Riley's thoughts back to the matter at hand. ''Sebastian McCullough. Your Mr. McCullough has a prison record.''

''For what?'' Riley asked and leaned forward in his chair.

''Domestic abuse. Seems Sebastian liked to beat up his wife.''

''He's married?'' Caralie asked in surprise.

''Not anymore. Divorced for five years. His wife divorced him while he was serving time for breaking her jaw. He's been clean since getting out of prison, but there've been several investigations into his work. He's very successful at playing the market, and there's speculation that he deals on insider tips.''

Riley slowly digested this new information as his gaze met Caralie's. ''Maybe Loretta found evidence of illegal trades and Sebastian silenced her for good.''

"Or maybe it's as we suspected before—his love for Loretta turned to rage." Caralie frowned thoughtfully and rubbed two fingers across the center of her forehead. "He has a history of violence so it wouldn't be out of character for him to set a fire."

"Wait, I'm not finished yet," Stanley interrupted their speculation. "Moving on to Tommy of Tommy's Tavern." Stanley shuffled through his papers. "Thomas Rhinegold a.k.a. Tommy the Terrible. Although Tommy has no criminal record, he's well-known to law enforcement. The police believe Tommy conducts a thriving drug trade through his tavern, but so far, despite dozens of sting operations, they haven't been able to pin anything on him." He looked at Riley, then at Caralie. "Drugs are a dirty business and people are often killed for threatening a prosperous operation."

Riley frowned. "I don't think our questions are threatening any drug operation."

"Why?" Caralie asked.

He looked at her solemnly. "Because if that were the case, we'd already be dead."

"I agree," Stanley said. "Drug dealers generally don't mess around with threats and warnings. They take care of a problem immediately and with a frightening finality."

Caralie sighed. "So, who is left?"

"Ah, that takes us to our illustrious mayor." Stanley rubbed the top of his bald head, as if rearranging hair that wasn't there. "Word is that Michael Monroe is very ambitious. He's hoping for a presidential appointment to some committee very soon and apparently is in politics for the long haul.''

''There's nothing criminal about being ambitious,'' Riley observed.

''True, but there's something unethical about running on a platform of marriage, commitment and family, then playing around on the side.'' Stanley grinned and rubbed his head once again. ''Rumor has it that Mayor Monroe likes females—preferably ones that aren't his wife. But unfortunately, there's nothing substantial to back up the rumors.''

Riley frowned, disappointed by what Stanley had to offer them. He wasn't sure what he'd expected, but it wasn't rumor and innuendo. ''So, we have two nice nurses, a man who has a criminal background and a politician who likes to play around on his wife.''

''We have one more thing,'' Stanley announced, his eyes twinkling brightly. ''We have the real name and the address of your mysterious Goldilocks.'' He grinned widely at the two of them. ''I'm good, right?''

Adrenaline shot through Riley. ''Oh, you're good. You're very good. So, what's her name and what's her story?''

''Her name is Paula Cantrell. She's twenty-four years old although she looks like she's about fifteen.''

''Well, who is she? What does she do?'' Caralie stood and paced the floor between the two men. The flowered skirt she wore swirled around her legs with a whispery swish, the sound and the sensual movement of her hips distracting Riley.

"Sit down, Caralie, and let Stanley finish," he said, his tone more curt than he'd intended.

She flopped back onto the sofa. "Was she friends with Loretta? Or is it possible she had something to do with Loretta's death?" She bit her bottom lip in an apparent effort to stop the flow of questions.

"I don't have all those answers," Stanley replied, his voice gentle with apology as he looked at Caralie. "I can tell you she works as a waitress at a little dive near where she lives and she worked at Tommy's Tavern about the same time your sister did."

Caralie closed her eyes and Riley knew what she was thinking. Finally, a place where answers might be possible. Finally, a person who might be able to tell them what had been going on in Loretta's life at the time of her death.

Stanley gave Riley the paperwork he'd compiled, along with the address of Paula Cantrell. "What do I owe you?" Riley asked as they walked him to the door.

"Nothing—except the facts, if this turns out to be a juicy news story."

"Thanks, Stanley, you've got it," Riley promised. The two men shook hands at the door, then Stanley turned to Caralie. "I hope you find the answers you're looking for. Maybe the information I dug up will get you that much closer."

"Yes, I think it will. Thank you, Stanley," she said.

With a bow to Caralie and a wink at Riley, Stanley left.

Instantly Caralie clutched Riley's arm, her eyes shining with excitement. "Oh, Riley...this is it. I know it, I feel it in my heart."

"I think you might be right," he agreed, trying to ignore how desirable she looked at the moment, with her eyes luminous and her face lit with anticipation.

She squeezed his arm tightly. "Finally...finally we're going to find out what happened to Loretta and who is responsible."

"So, what are you waiting for?" he teased. "Grab your coat and let's go find out exactly what our Ms. Goldilocks knows."

It wasn't until they were on their way to Goldilocks's house that Riley realized his feelings about talking to the young woman were oddly ambivalent. If Paula Cantrell possessed the answers Caralie sought, then the first part of Caralie's quest was complete and she was one step closer to moving out of his life. This thought alone caused a peculiar, unexpected pang in his heart.

But the real question was, Would she move out of his life alone, or would she take the child he loved with her?

Chapter Eleven

Caralie's heart pounded in her chest as she and Riley left his house. Hopefully she would soon learn not only exactly what had happened to Loretta, but why it had happened.

"What are you doing?" she asked as Riley headed toward the downtown section of Houston. Paula Cantrell lived in one of the two apartment buildings they had staked out several nights before, but Riley was now driving in the opposite direction.

"Last time we were in the area of Goldilocks's house, we were attacked. I think I saw two men in that car—two 'bears.' I figure this time we'll be smarter and try a few diversionary tactics to throw off anyone who might be following us."

"You think we're being followed?" Caralie twisted around in the seat to look behind them.

Riley chuckled. "If we're being followed you won't be able to spot them just by looking back unless they are idiots. It might be enough that we're in a different car, but I'm not willing to take chances."

The day before, Riley had taken his damaged car

into the shop and Caralie had talked him into using her rental until his was fixed. Her rental had been parked in Riley's garage and Caralie hoped that meant whoever might be after them wouldn't be aware that she and Riley had the compact car.

She twined and untwined her hands together in her lap, filled with a restless energy impossible to contain. It was almost over. The haunting questions concerning Loretta's death might finally be answered. And then Caralie could move forward with her life.

She frowned and stared out the passenger-side window. What life? She had no home, no job, and now that she'd decided she couldn't marry David, she had no idea what to expect in the future.

If they learned today why Loretta had died and who was responsible, it would be time to move out of Riley's home and start the proceedings that would give her custody of Kaycee.

For the first time since she'd arrived at Riley's door, doubts assailed Caralie. Was it really the right thing to do—to take Kaycee away from the father she had bonded with, the father who adored her?

But it was what Loretta wanted, she reminded herself. And it was what she needed. She needed Kaycee in her life—somebody to love without reservation; a child who would love her and never walk away.

"There's no guarantee that this Paula knows everything we're trying to find out." Riley's voice broke into Caralie's thoughts.

"I know. But she knows something. Why else would she have run from you that night at Chubbie's?"

He grinned at her, his dimple flashing like an unexpected gift. ''Maybe she just didn't like my looks.''

Caralie smiled, knowing his stab at humor was an attempt to ease some of the tension that coiled inside her. ''I doubt if there are too many women who run in revulsion when you approach.''

Her smile faded as she continued to study his features. As always, the sight of Riley created a warm pool of pleasure inside her. Her feelings for him were more complicated than mere physical attraction, although that, in itself, was incredibly strong.

He turned his head and caught her thoughtful gaze. ''Have I suddenly grown a horn in my forehead?'' he asked teasingly.

She flushed, embarrassed to have been caught staring. ''I... No...I was just thinking that if we find out what happened to Loretta today, then it will be time for me to move out of your place.''

He didn't answer for a long moment. ''There's no real hurry,'' he finally said. He pulled the car in against the curb. ''I mean, you aren't any real trouble and you don't eat much. Even if we get answers to everything today, that doesn't mean you need to be in a big hurry to move out. No sense in you moving back to a motel. You're welcome to stay until you find an appropriate place to live.''

Again she felt the pool of warmth, this time larger, deeper; drowning depths that frightened her. ''Thank you,'' she said, touched by his generous hospitality, especially in light of the fact that eventually they would be on opposite sides of a court case.

He turned off the car engine. "From here we'll take a couple of city buses, make it really difficult for anyone to tail us."

"This all feels so ridiculously clandestine," Caralie said moments later as they took seats on a crowded bus.

"It feels smart," Riley replied.

"At least you aren't making me wear a pair of funny glasses and a fake nose."

He laughed. "That's plan B."

They changed buses twice, then got off at the corner where they had parked to stake out the apartments earlier in the week.

"That one," Riley said, pointing to the tall brick building on the left side of the street. He took her by the elbow and led her across the intersection and through the entrance of the old building.

There were two apartment doors on the left, two down the hall on the right, and a bank of elevators directly in front of them. "We go up," Riley said. "According to Stanley, she lives in apartment 1404."

The elevator smelled of stale air and moved upward with a series of jerks and groans. Anticipation once again soared through Caralie. Answers. She desperately needed answers, and hopefully within the next few minutes she would have them.

With success so close, she fought the impulse to wrap her arms around Riley's neck, tell him how grateful she was for his help, confess that somehow, someway he had managed to gain a foothold in her heart. But, her feelings frightened her. She didn't want to care for Riley.

The elevator thudded to a halt and the doors whooshed open. Any momentary thoughts of her feelings about Riley fell aside as they stepped out of the elevator and approached the door of apartment 1404.

"She might not talk to us," Riley warned.

"She has to," Caralie said fervently. "She's the only real link we have to Loretta. Somehow I'll make her tell us everything she knows."

Riley looked at her for a long moment, his gaze gentle. "You know you might not like what you hear about Loretta's life-style."

Caralie nodded. Yes, she had already reconciled herself to that fact. When Sebastian had mentioned that he had initially thought Loretta might have been a prostitute, Caralie had been shocked.

However, that shock had transformed into an uneasy realization that Loretta had had the emotional makeup to become a prostitute; that she'd been a woman who had desperately needed love.

As Riley knocked on the door, he grabbed Caralie's hand, as if offering her strength. She curled her fingers around his as they stood and waited for a reply to the knock.

Long, agonizing moments passed without an answer. Riley knocked again, this time louder, and they both heard a muffled acknowledgment from within. Another minute passed before they heard the sound of a dead bolt being turned. The door opened about two inches, a guard chain in place as a pair of blue eyes peered out, then widened in horror.

"Go away!" she exclaimed, and slammed the door shut.

"Wait!" Caralie released Riley's hand and banged on the door. "Paula...please. We just want to talk to you."

"I don't want to talk to you," she cried, her voice half hysterical. "For God's sake, just go!"

"But you don't understand—I'm Loretta Tracey's sister. I know you were her friend. Please...please just let us ask you some questions." Caralie banged on the door with both fists, tears of frustration blurring her vision.

"Paula, we aren't here to cause trouble," Riley added.

"But you *are* causing me trouble just by being here!" she screamed through the wooden barrier of the door. "Just get the hell out of here! I have nothing to say to you. I can't help you in any way. I don't know anything. Please...just go away and leave me alone!" Her words still rang through the empty hallway as a piece of paper appeared beneath her door.

Riley bent down and picked up the note, scanned it quickly, then handed it to Caralie.

Can't Talk Here—Danger. Eyes And Ears Everywhere. Meet Tonight at Tommy's Tavern. Midnight.

Caralie read the note, then looked around, the nape of her neck tingling as if she were being watched.

''Eyes and ears everywhere'' What did that mean? *Whose* eyes and ears were watching? Listening?

''Go on...get out of here before I call the cops and charge you with harassment!'' Paula yelled through the door. ''I'm not talking to you and that's that.''

''I guess she can't help us,'' Riley said, eyeing Caralie pointedly. He took the note from her and pocketed it. ''Come on, we're wasting our time here.''

They didn't speak another word until they were once again on a city bus heading back toward where Riley had parked the car.

''Do you think somebody was in there with her?'' Caralie asked. She and Riley stood facing one another, their bodies so close that each bump in the road created intimate contact.

''No. If somebody had been there she couldn't have written the note.'' He reached out to steady her as the bus careened around a corner. ''But she's obviously scared and afraid somebody is watching her, maybe listening to her.''

''I'm going to go crazy waiting for midnight,'' Caralie said.

Riley smiled, his dimple flashing momentarily. ''At least you won't go crazy alone. I'll be right with you.''

Caralie nodded and averted her gaze from his, and tried to ignore his closeness, the way his familiar scent surrounded her. His body radiated a sweet heat that engulfed her and she realized she wanted to make love with him again.

In recognizing her desire for him, she also acknowledged that somehow, someway, she had fallen in love with him.

Her pulse raced and her mouth went dry as the sudden knowledge penetrated her mind, seeped into the core of her heart. God help her, she'd fallen helplessly, hopelessly in love with Wild Man Riley Kincaid. And that love threatened and frightened her more than anything the mysterious Paula might tell them that night about Loretta.

BY THE TIME THEY returned home, it was after five. Riley ordered in pizza for dinner, knowing neither of them was in the mood to cook.

Caralie had been silent on the drive home and Riley assumed she was preoccupied with thoughts of her sister and the anticipation of finally having the answers she needed. And when she got those answers, she would go—walk out of his life and leave behind an empty place where her presence had once been.

He put on a pot of coffee, then sat at the table to await the pizza delivery. Moments before, Caralie had disappeared into her bedroom, mumbling something about changing clothes.

He closed his eyes and imagined her in the bedroom, heard the soft hiss of her zipper as it slid down, the sound of fabric whispering against skin as her dress slipped to the floor. His hands clenched as he imagined touching her skin so creamy, so soft. His fingers remembered the tactile pleasure of stroking her, his nose held the memory of the sweet fragrance of her.

His jeans suddenly felt too tight, constricting him as desire swelled within. He stood in an effort to find comfort, but knew there was only one thing that would give him that—Caralie.

''Riley?''

He whirled at the sound of her voice. She stood in the doorway, clad in a pair of light blue sweatpants and a matching sweatshirt. Her hair was loose and tumbled around her shoulders like a silken cloak. She'd never looked as lovely, and desire rocketed through Riley.

She must have seen it in his eyes—the fire that burned within him. Her eyes flared wide and she moistened her lips with the tip of her tongue. ''Did you order the pizza?'' she asked, her voice unusually husky.

''Yeah. It should be here in about an hour.'' He was aware that his voice matched hers, deeper than usual, filled with suppressed emotion.

''An hour?'' she echoed, her feet carrying her closer to him.

He nodded and took several steps forward, meeting her in the center of the kitchen, standing so close to her he could feel her breath on his neck, felt the heat that emanated from her. ''Caralie.'' Her name was a song that tripped from his lips, holding all the longing, all the desire that soared through his soul.

She closed her eyes with a soft intake of breath. When she opened them again they were a smoldering, deep gray. "Yes," she whispered, answering the question he realized he'd asked. She tilted her head up, offering her lips for him to claim.

And he did. He covered her mouth with his in a fiery kiss as he pulled her tightly against the length of his body. She molded to him—her softness to his hardness. She returned his kiss with a matching hunger, her hands tangling in his hair as she pressed intimately against him.

Somewhere in the back of his mind, Riley knew they shouldn't be touching, shouldn't be kissing each other. She intended to marry another man, and was resolved to battle him for the little girl he loved.

But, even knowing they were on the road to a mistake, he couldn't stop. He wanted to fall into her and remain there forever, linger indefinitely in her silken caresses, revel in her sweet, fevered sighs.

"Oh, yes," she murmured as his lips left hers and trailed down the side of her neck, lingered in the hollow of her throat.

"I want you," he whispered as he felt her heartbeat quicken to a matching rhythm of his own.

"I want you, too. I want to feel you beside me...inside me."

Her words stoked his internal fire higher, hotter. "But not here," he said. He scooped her up in his arms. "I want you in my bed."

He carried her to his room. Once there, they shed their clothes and fell onto the bed in a fevered embrace. Riley couldn't get enough of her. He loved her taste, her scent, the way she looked in the kiss of the golden twilight that seeped through the window and played on her skin.

There was no shyness between them. They gave and took, fingers touching, mouths tasting, bodies moving in unselfconscious togetherness.

Riley had sensed a well of passion deep within Caralie. He'd tapped into it the first time they'd made love and again, this time, he felt her abandoning control and giving in to her natural instincts.

She was ready for him, wet and hot, when he finally slipped inside her. Tears sparkled on her lashes as she urged him deeper within. He knew they weren't tears of pain, nor tears of regret, but rather the manifestation of sheer emotion. He knew this because he felt a burning behind his own eyelids—the sheer, unadulterated emotion of joy and completeness as he possessed her totally.

They clung to each other long after they had both reached their climax, as if reluctant to break their physical connection.

Riley stroked her hair, then on down the length of her bare back, and felt a wholeness of spirit he'd experienced only once before—with a woman who had died and left him to face life alone.

Was it possible he was falling in love with Caralie? His hand paused mid-stroke through her hair as he contemplated this thought. The day he'd buried Angela, he'd promised himself he would never again fall in love, never again place himself in a position to grieve the loss of a beloved.

But those had been the vows of a boy suffering his first heartache, the pledge of youth unable to see any future beyond the pain of the moment. It had taken Kaycee to mend his shattered heart. Would Caralie be the one to break it once again?

The doorbell rang. Riley jumped up and grabbed his robe. "That will be the pizza," he said.

Caralie smiled and stretched languidly, her sensual movement reawakening a burst of desire inside him. "It's a good thing it didn't arrive thirty minutes earlier."

"Or thirty minutes later," he replied, knowing his gaze held a promise of what might come.

She blushed. "Go get the pizza. I'm starving."

By the time he'd paid for the pizza and brought it into the kitchen, Caralie was there, once again fully dressed, as if to ward off any thoughts he might have of a repeat performance.

When he approached the table, he could tell she'd distanced herself emotionally from him. She was gazing at the clock on the oven. "Five and a half hours to midnight," she said.

Riley nodded, slightly disconcerted by how easily she'd transformed from the passionate, giving woman who'd been in his bed to this cool, collected woman who looked at him so dispassionately.

In the years since Angela, Riley had always managed to maintain his emotional distance from the women he'd slept with, but this time was different. Caralie was different. And this time was different because Riley was in love. He wondered what she would do if he told her he loved her; if he asked her to forget "Saint" David and take a chance on him.

But, as he gazed at her face, saw the distraction

he knew was caused by the pending midnight meeting, he knew that now was not the time to talk of love and choices. After they'd met with Paula, after they'd obtained some answers to Loretta's life and death, there would be time to talk of love.

With this thought in mind, he asked her the important question of the moment: ''Mushroom or pepperoni?''

Chapter Twelve

It was just after eleven when Riley and Caralie left the house through a window in the studio. Riley, concerned that his place was being watched, had decided they should sneak out and walk two blocks to an all-night grocery store where he would phone for a taxi to pick them up.

As they waited for the cab that would take them to their rendezvous at Tommy's Tavern, Caralie tried to keep her thoughts away from Riley and focused on the meeting to come. But no matter how much she tried to avoid them, images of Riley and their recent lovemaking intruded.

She knew she would never make love with him again. Their early-evening passion would never be repeated.

She couldn't. Her heart was becoming far too entangled with his, and she refused to allow herself to fall any more deeply in love with him. She had to protect herself. She refused to be weak like Loretta—always needing a man to validate herself. She'd be fine alone. All she needed was Kaycee.

She frowned, assailed by doubts as she thought of taking Kaycee out of Riley's custody. She wanted what was right and good for the child. Initially, she'd believed with all her heart that Kaycee's best interests would be served by removing her from Riley's custody. She was no longer certain of that fact.

With a squeal of tires, the taxi pulled up at the curb and she and Riley climbed into the back. Caralie stared out the window into the darkness of the night, tugging her thoughts away from the custody issue and back to what the night might bring.

"You know Tommy's Tavern on the south side of town?" Riley asked the driver. He nodded. "Drive us around for about fifteen minutes, then take us to Tommy's."

As the taxi shot forward, Caralie was aware of Riley's gaze on her. "We look like a couple of cat burglars," he said, indicating the dark clothing they'd agreed to wear.

Caralie offered him a small smile. "Climbing out of windows, camouflaging ourselves to blend with the night—I hope the information Paula has to give us is worth all the trouble."

She sighed. "I need this to be over. I need to move on with my life. I feel as if everything has been on hold since the moment I heard about Loretta's death."

Riley's hand covered hers and she knew he meant to give her comfort. But his touch didn't comfort; it tormented. And she knew she had to stop living in his home, had to get away from him. Somehow, she had to stop loving him.

"Tonight is the end of it," she said, speaking part of her thoughts aloud. Riley's eyes narrowed at her words. "I've got to put this all behind me and move forward. Whatever Paula tells us tonight, it has to be enough for me."

He nodded. "You have to do what's right for you."

And she knew that "right" for her was to get away from Riley, before her heart was forever scarred and broken. He would always be in her life through their common love of Loretta's child, but Caralie knew she could never again allow him to kiss her, encourage him to make love to her, without paying too high a price.

She'd allowed Riley's passion to sway her from her initial responsibility. She cast him a surreptitious glance. Was that what he'd intended to do? To seduce her into forgetting to fight for custody? Riley might be many things, but she didn't believe—couldn't believe—that he would stoop that low. No. She'd tasted sweet passion on his lips—not exploitation, not manufactured desire to gain an upper hand.

Caralie had to remain strong and focused on her goals. Loretta had written to Caralie that she didn't want Kaycee's father to have custody, that she wanted Caralie to parent the little girl. Caralie couldn't deny her sister this request, no matter how sweet Riley's kisses. She had to do what Loretta had asked of her, even if it broke Riley's heart—and even if her own got broken in the process.

The cab braking to a stop pulled her from her

thoughts. She realized they'd arrived at Tommy's Tavern. Riley and Caralie climbed out of the back seat and Riley leaned into the passenger-side window and threw a bill toward the driver. "Drive one block down and wait for us," he instructed.

The cabbie threw the money back at him. "Russ told me to do whatever you needed...no charge."

Riley tucked the bill into his back pocket with a solemn nod. "I don't know how long we'll be."

The driver shrugged. "I got all night."

Riley and Caralie watched as he pulled down the street, then parked against the curb. Riley turned to Caralie, his eyes glittering with anticipation and a dark edge of danger. "Stay close to me," he instructed as he took her arm and pulled her to his side. "We don't know what we're walking into."

For the first time since talking to Paula that afternoon, Caralie realized the possibility of danger. They knew nothing about the woman they were meeting. She and Riley had been forced off the road, their names had been scrawled on headstones. It was possible that Paula was setting them up for an ambush with the very men who'd been threatening them.

"Ready?" Riley's hand squeezed her arm.

"Yes...no... Riley, what if this is a setup?"

"The possibility crossed my mind." He smiled tightly and lifted his dark sweatshirt enough for her to see a handgun tucked in his waistband. "Did you really think Wild Man Riley wouldn't be prepared for anything?" He allowed his shirt to drop down, covering the weapon again.

A new burst of fear flooded Caralie at the sight of

the gun. Again she was reminded that this was no game, and there were no rules; if Loretta had really been murdered, then the guilty would probably do anything to keep that fact from coming to light... including killing again.

"Let's go," Riley said as he looked at his watch. "It's exactly midnight."

The interior of the tavern was smoky and loud, filled with people who crowded around the bar, sat at the scarred tables or yelled and cursed as they shot pool.

Riley didn't have to prompt her again to stick close to him. As he walked toward the bar, Caralie glued herself to his side, her hand clutching his arm. Tommy saw their approach and pointed to a door to the left of the long, wooden bar, his expression inscrutable.

As they neared the doorway, Caralie felt Riley's muscles tense, saw the tic in his jaw begin a rhythmic beat. He looked as dangerous as anyone they might encounter on the other side of the door.

Riley eased the door open and peered inside, his gaze narrowed in concentration. He looked at Caralie and nodded, and together they stepped through the doorway and into a small back storage room.

Large boxes containing bottles of liquor were stacked from floor to ceiling, small paths between the boxes led to metal shelves that held packages of napkins, glassware and cleaning supplies.

Riley moved his hand and gripped his weapon as he and Caralie stood in the center of the room, waiting for whatever was to come. "Anyone here?" he called softly.

There was a rustling sound from behind one of the piles of boxes. Caralie tensed as Riley pulled his gun and pointed it in the direction of the noise.

Goldilocks stepped into view. "For God's sake, put that thing away before somebody gets hurt!" she exclaimed. Riley, apparently not satisfied there was no danger, lowered the barrel but kept the gun firmly in hand.

For a moment the three of them simply looked at each other, tension palpable in the air. Up close, Goldilocks a.k.a. Paula Cantrell wasn't as young as Caralie had initially thought her. Although her long, golden hair and big blue eyes gave her an aura of youth, there were lines radiating from her eyes and on either side of her mouth. She looked older than the twenty-four years Stanley had reported her to be.

Paula sank onto a stray box on the floor and expelled a deep sigh. "You don't realize the danger you've put me in by coming around my place."

"We didn't mean to put you in danger," Caralie replied. "But we need some answers about my sister, and you're our only lead. You knew her, right?"

"Knew her? Loretta was my best friend." Paula's eyes welled up with tears. She swiped at them angrily and pointed a finger at Riley. "Could you lose the gun? We're safe here. Tommy won't let anyone come back here that might be a problem."

Riley stared at Paula, then looked at Caralie. "Why should we trust her?"

Caralie gazed at Paula, wishing she could see into

the woman's heart. She finally turned to Riley and shrugged. "Because we don't have anyone else to trust."

He tucked the gun back into his pants and Caralie eased down to sit on a box across from Paula. "Tell us everything you know. You talked of danger—danger from who?"

Paula plucked at one of her pale eyebrows, her hand trembling slightly. "In order for you to understand everything, I've got to start at the beginning, when I first met your sister."

Caralie nodded encouragingly.

"I started working here with Loretta right after you'd left the States. She was depressed. She didn't know many people here and was afraid she couldn't pay the rent on her apartment by herself, so she invited me to move in with her." Paula ran a finger over her eyebrow, then laced her hands together in her lap.

"Who are you afraid of? Why did you run from us that night we saw you in Chubbie's?" Riley asked in an obvious attempt to hurry her along.

Paula frowned. "I got to tell this my own way," she replied. "It's the only way it all makes sense."

"Go on," Caralie prompted, although like Riley she wanted to get to the pertinent information. What had happened to her sister and who exactly was responsible?

"Anyway, Loretta and I lived together and things were going pretty good. We were a lot alike and we had good times together." Paula smiled, as if remembering those times. Her smile faded. "Then she met somebody. She wouldn't tell me who he was—said it was a secret.''

Paula looked almost wistful. ''She seemed so happy. She believed she'd finally met her Prince Charming and all the bad times were behind her.''

''So what happened?'' Riley asked as he leaned against a stack of boxes.

''For a while things seemed to be terrific. She quit working here and moved out into a big fancy apartment, said her boyfriend wanted her to have the best of everything—and that's what she had. I visited her there a couple of times but it felt weird. She wouldn't tell me who the man was, had so many secrets, so I quit coming around.''

Caralie swallowed each morsel of information, her heart aching for her sister, who'd once again given her life over to a man, relinquished control both financially and probably spiritually, in an effort to be loved.

''Then, out of the blue she called me, told me she'd broken up with her boyfriend, who'd promised her marriage but refused to get divorced from his wife. She told me she was dating a photographer.'' Paula looked at Riley. ''She thought you were a nice guy, but she knew you weren't in the market for anything permanent.''

Riley nodded, his dark eyes not meeting Caralie's. She knew he probably felt as guilty as she did—as if somehow, someway, they had all let Loretta down.

''Anyway, the next thing I know she's back with her married lover and certain that everything is going to work out just fine. And that's when she told me the name of the man.'' Paula looked at them both expectantly.

''Who?'' Caralie asked, knowing that whoever Loretta had been involved with was also involved in her death.

''Michael Monroe. Mayor Michael Monroe.''

THE NAME HUNG IN the air.

Shock coursed through Riley. He'd played and replayed different possibilities in his mind, had wondered if Loretta had stumbled on a drug connection and Tommy had set the fire to silence her. Or perhaps she'd toyed with Sebastian and in a jealous fit he'd killed her.

But he hadn't really considered the possibility that the mayor was involved in any way—that Loretta might have been killed to save a political career.

''Are you sure?'' Caralie's voice was a mere whisper and Riley knew she felt the same breathless shock that he did.

Paula nodded. ''Positive. It was Mayor Monroe who set her up in the apartment, paid all her bills and kept her like a pet dog. And it's Mayor Monroe's two goon bodyguards who have been making my life hell ever since Loretta died in that fire.''

Tears once again sparkled on Paula's pale lashes. ''They knew I knew about Loretta and the mayor, and for several months after her death, they hounded me, threatening that if I opened my mouth I'd be sorry.'' The tears spilled down her cheeks and she swiped at them with the back of her hand. ''I knew what they'd done to Loretta so I didn't take their threats lightly. After a couple of weeks the threats stopped and I didn't see the goons hanging around anymore. Then you two started digging up stuff and the threats started again.'' She glared at them both.

''But you've got to tell somebody what you know!'' Caralie exclaimed. ''You have to go to the police.''

''Oh yeah, right.'' Paula emitted a sarcastic laugh. ''I might be a natural blonde, but I'm not natural stupid. Guess who has the police department in his back pocket? Guess who plays golf every Wednesday afternoon with the chief of police? Yeah, right...our illustrious mayor.''

Riley felt Caralie's frustration, but knew Paula spoke the truth. The political machinery would rip them up if they tried to take this information through the police department. ''She's right, Caralie. Going to the police isn't an option.''

Caralie jumped up from where she'd been sitting. ''But there has to be something we can do. He has to pay. I don't give a damn who he is.''

Riley frowned thoughtfully. ''I'm not sure I understand all this. Loretta and Michael Monroe were having an affair. So why would he kill her?''

Caralie stared at him, then turned and looked at Paula. ''Yes...why would he kill her? If he wanted to end the affair, why not just end it?''

''I think he tried to. Then Loretta started threatening him. She told him if he didn't divorce his wife and make good on his promises to her, she'd go to the press.''

''But that shouldn't have threatened him,'' Riley

argued. Caralie looked at him quizzically. "We went through all her paperwork. There was nothing to connect her with the mayor. The transactions for the apartment were all handled in cash. She would have had no proof. It would have been his word against hers."

"But she did have proof," Paula protested. "She had the—baby—*his* baby."

All the air in Riley's lungs expelled as if he'd been hit hard in the solar plexus. He was vaguely aware of Caralie's gasp, but he couldn't focus on her. Shock and pain rippled through him as he struggled to regain his breath. No. Not Kaycee. Oh please, God. It couldn't be true. Kaycee was his, not Monroe's.

As air seeped back into his lungs, he became aware of Caralie and Paula both staring at him—Paula in confusion and Caralie in weary sadness.

"No." The word escaped him without volition. "She's mine. The time of her birth is right. Loretta named me on the birth certificate. She's mine." His voice rose in strength, daring either woman to contradict him.

Paula shrugged. "I can only tell you that by the time Loretta went to the hospital to give birth, she was terrified of Michael Monroe. She'd rather have written down Attila the Hun as the father than name him on the birth certificate."

Riley felt as if he were dying. Piece by piece, bit by bit, his soul withered as he thought of the little girl he loved more than life. *It doesn't matter,* he told himself. *It doesn't matter if she came from my seed or not. She's my daughter. She's mine!*

And yet he knew it did matter. If Kaycee was Monroe's child, then Riley had no ammunition to fight Caralie for custody. He was nothing more than an interested third party with no blood ties to give him any advantage.

"That's all I can tell you, and I'll never speak of any of this again." Paula stood and flipped her hair behind her shoulders, seemingly unaware that she had shattered Riley's very soul.

She looked at Caralie. "I loved Loretta like a sister, so I figured I owed it to her to tell you what I knew. But this is where it ends for me. I'm leaving town in the next week. I'm moving someplace where I don't have to look over my shoulder."

Riley listened absently as the two spoke a little longer about Loretta. Their words barely penetrated the fog that had engulfed him the moment he'd realized his daughter might not actually be his. The very foundation of the world he'd built with Kaycee had been shaken and he didn't know how to regain his footing.

"I'll go first. You two wait ten minutes or so, then you can leave," Paula said, the words indicating to Riley that their meeting had come to an end.

As Riley watched, Paula slipped out the door and disappeared. He stared at the closed door, unable to believe that in a matter of minutes, she'd destroyed his life, then calmly walked away.

"Riley?" Caralie's voice was soft, gentle. He started as she laid a hand on his arm. He looked at her, saw the sadness, the deep sympathy that darkened her eyes. "We don't know for sure...."

He clenched his fists, fighting to maintain control

over his tumultuous emotions. "Come on, let's get out of here." He took her by the elbow and propelled her out the door and into the smoky confines of the bar.

He glanced neither left nor right, focused only on the door that would take him outside and into the fresh night air. He needed to clear his head, rationally dissect what Paula had said and how it affected him.

He and Caralie didn't speak on the way home. Riley was too heartsick to form words. Even if Kaycee was Monroe's child, it wouldn't change Riley's love for her. Nothing could make him stop loving Kaycee.

However, he knew that if Paula was right—if Kaycee really was Monroe's biological child—then he'd lose her. And it was this thought that absolutely broke his heart.

"You want to talk about it?" Caralie asked, once they were back in his house.

Riley sank down on the sofa and buried his head in his hands. "I don't even want to think about it," he murmured truthfully.

"Riley...I promise you'll get liberal visitation." She spoke the words softly and he knew she meant to ease his pain, but it was as if she'd driven a nail into an open wound.

He raised his head and stared at her—not angry with her, but enraged by the entire situation. "You haven't won yet. Like I said before, the timing is right for her to be mine. I'm not going to roll over and play dead just because some woman I don't even know told us some story."

He stood, a burst of renewed hope flooding

through him. ''I'll get a DNA test done. That will settle the issue. Then we'll see where we are.'' Neither of them spoke of what might happen if it was proved that Michael Monroe was the father and he then decided to fight them both for custody.

A knot of anger twisted in Riley's stomach. He'd make sure that Michael Monroe never gained custody of Kaycee, and he knew Caralie would fight that particular scenario, as well. Besides, it would never happen. Kaycee was his—*his!* ''A DNA test will answer any question about Kaycee's paternity.''

Caralie nodded slowly. ''Okay.''

''So, what are you going to do now?'' he asked.

She frowned. ''I know I said that no matter what happened tonight, no matter what I learned, it was finished. But, I can't let it go. I don't know what to do, I don't know how, but Michael Monroe needs to pay for what he did.''

''But you know going to the police is out of the question.''

Her frown deepened and she tucked a strand of hair behind her ear. ''I know, but if I let it go, he's getting away with murder. And no matter what happens, he'll never, *never* get Kaycee.''

Her eyes glittered with the promise of tears. ''He killed my sister,'' she whispered, her words thick with emotion. ''All she did was love him and he killed her.''

As she began to cry, Riley shoved his own heartache away, knowing that at the moment she needed his arms around her, needed his support to ease the ache in her heart. And he couldn't deny her. Despite the fact that he knew she'd fight him for Kaycee, he loved her too much to remain distant at the flood of her tears.

He eased down next to her on the sofa and wrapped her in his arms. He held her close, allowing the front of his shirt to soak up her grief. He didn't speak, knew there were no words that would comfort her. She needed this final cry for the sister she'd lost.

As she wept, a plan began to formulate in his mind—a plan that would make Mayor Michael Monroe accountable for his sins, perhaps answerable for his crimes.

When her tears ended, he told her of his scheme, watched her eyes light with the possibility of vindication. "It's late," he finally said. "We can talk more about it in the morning."

He stood and held out his hand to her. She allowed him to pull her up off the sofa and together they walked to her bedroom. "It will all work out, Caralie," he said. "He'll pay. One way or another, we'll make sure he pays."

She nodded wearily. "Good night, Riley."

He kissed her on the forehead. "Good night, Caralie."

She disappeared into her bedroom and closed the door behind her. Riley started toward his own room, but at the last minute detoured into the nursery.

He switched on the dim lamp on the dresser and sank down in the rocking chair next to the crib. He still remembered that moment when the nurse had first placed Kaycee in his arms. She'd mewled like a newborn kitten, then opened her eyes and gazed at him soberly. In that instant a bond had been forged—a bond of love that nothing could break.

Moving his legs, he rocked back and forth, thinking of all the nights he'd sat here, holding her close and humming nonsensical tunes to put her to sleep. Each milestone was etched in his mind—the day she rolled over, the evening when she first sat up by herself; the first tooth, the first smile, the first giggle.

He wanted to hate Caralie for threatening to take his baby away, but he couldn't. He couldn't hate her because he loved her. He knew she was only acting in the best interests of Kaycee and following her sister's final wishes. In truth, he loved her more for doing just that.

Caralie. His love for her burned in his throat, ached in his chest. And now, it would appear to be the biggest form of manipulation for him to tell her of his love. Now she would believe any words of love from him were merely an effort to retain custody.

And so in the end, if the worst happened, he would lose not only Kaycee, but any hope for a future with Caralie, as well. Oh, God, he wished he was still Wild Man Riley, with his heart encased in stone. He wished he had the protection that had served him so well in the past. But that self-protection was gone, leaving him weak and vulnerable to the pain that roared through him.

Rocking back and forth, with the scent of Kaycee in the air and the memory of Caralie's sweet caresses in his heart, Riley wept.

Chapter Thirteen

The next morning Caralie found a note from Riley on the table. He'd gone to run errands and asked that she meet him at the Lone Star Motel at two o'clock.

It was already after ten. Caralie had overslept after a night of tossing and turning. She'd heard Riley in Kaycee's room, crying deep sobs of anguish. She'd wanted to go in and comfort him, but she didn't have any words of comfort, knew his pain was too deep for mere words to appease. She was also far too aware of her own role in Riley's pain, and her guilt and grief for him kept her away from him.

What a mess she'd created by coming into his life. His entire world had been destroyed by her appearance, with her questions and need for answers.

What a mess Loretta had left behind for them to sort out. Caralie wondered if any of them would be the same when it was all over.

The three bears—Michael Monroe and his two goon bodyguards. Michael Monroe—"papa bear." Now she understood Loretta's letter where she'd said the father didn't want to be involved. She understood why Loretta had said that if anything happened to her, she wanted Caralie to gain custody of the baby.

But why had Loretta named Riley as father on the birth certificate?

Was it possible Loretta hadn't known for sure which of the men had been the father? Was it possible Kaycee could be Riley's biological child? Even though Caralie knew that would complicate her custody case, she hoped it was so.

She mulled all this over for the remainder of the morning and early afternoon and it still played on her mind as she drove to the Lone Star Motel.

Perhaps Loretta had known for sure that Michael was Kaycee's father, but had named Riley on the birth certificate as protection, knowing Caralie would eventually get custody and raise the little girl.

It was all so confusing—and so heartbreaking. There seemed to be no easy answers, and no easy fix for the problems Loretta had left behind.

Caralie was still trying to sort through the information Paula had given them the night before as she pulled into the parking lot of the motel.

It seemed like a lifetime ago that she had rented a room here, anxious to meet the man who had been taking care of her sister's child, eager to connect with the baby Loretta had left behind. A lifetime ago when everything seemed far less complicated.

And now, there was a little girl's future at risk, danger everywhere and a man who'd managed to capture a large chunk of her heart.

She frowned as she pulled to a halt and eyed the connected units that comprised the motel rooms. Riley hadn't specified exactly where she was to meet him or why he'd wanted her to meet him here.

Just as Caralie was about to go to the office, Riley's mother, Margaret, stepped out of unit 108 and motioned to Caralie.

Surprised, Caralie pulled into the parking space in front of the older woman. She wondered what Margaret was doing here and what, if anything, Riley had told his mother of the events of the night before.

Did Margaret know that Riley might not be Kaycee's father? That Margaret might not be the little girl's biological grandmother?

Damn Michael Monroe. She gripped the steering wheel tightly and hoped he'd burn in the fiery flames of hell. He'd killed Loretta and probably felt smug about the fact that the crime had been concealed, that he would face no criminal charges.

Well, if Riley's plan worked, he still wouldn't face criminal charges, but he'd face something worse.

Drawing a deep breath, she got out of her car. "What a surprise," she greeted Margaret. "I thought you and Kaycee were in Kansas City."

"We were until this morning." Margaret motioned Caralie inside. "Riley called me early this morning and arranged for us to take an immediate flight back." She closed the door and locked it with both the dead bolt and the chain. "He made arrangements for us to stay here rather than at home for safety's sake."

She motioned Caralie into one of the chairs at the small table in front of the window where the draperies were drawn tightly closed. "I'd offer you something to drink, but there's nothing here except water."

"I'm fine," Caralie said as she sat down.

"Riley told me all about your meeting last night." Margaret sat across from Caralie. "I'm sorry about your sister. If it's any consolation, I didn't vote for Michael Monroe. Thought he was too slick, as charming as a poisonous snake."

A burst of warm affection for Margaret filled Caralie as she recognized Margaret's words as a sign of support. And with that affection came a surge of guilt for all the unhappiness she had brought. "I'm sorry about everything else...." She let her voice trail off, knowing Margaret would understand what she meant.

"Riley took Kaycee down to some lab to start the DNA testing."

Surprise filled Caralie. He'd certainly not wasted any time. Caralie's heart constricted as she realized how hard the entire situation was on him, and on Margaret.

"It's just as well we know," Margaret continued matter-of-factly. "Of course, it won't make any difference in the way we feel about Kaycee," she added hurriedly. "Still, I suppose we need to know for future medical questions that might come up." Her voice lacked conviction and Caralie knew the older woman's heart was breaking just like Riley's.

"You must hate me," Caralie said, lacing her hands tightly together in front of her. "I mean, I showed up here and really complicated your lives.

You can't even stay in the comfort of your own home because of me and my curiosity.''

''Should I hate you for wanting to find out exactly what happened to your sister? Or for wanting to do what's best for her child?'' Margaret shook her head. ''No, I don't hate you...although I must confess I fear you more than a little.''

''Fear me?'' Caralie eyed Margaret in surprise. ''You mean because you're afraid I'll take Kaycee and deny you an opportunity to be her grandmother?''

''No.'' Margaret waved a hand dismissively. ''I don't believe you're heartless—and that would be a cold, heartless thing to do.'' She paused for a moment, stared at the ugly dark green drapes, then looked back at Caralie, her gaze intent.

''No, I fear you because I think you have the power to break my son's heart.''

''No matter what happens with the DNA testing and the custody issue, I'll always make sure Riley gets liberal visitation with Kaycee,'' Caralie said fervently, knowing she could never, ever deprive Kaycee of Riley's love.

''I'm not talking about the custody issue. I'm talking about the fact that my son is in love with you.''

Caralie felt the blood leave her face at Margaret's unexpected words. ''Oh, no...no, you're mistaken,'' she protested.

''My dear, if there's one thing I know, it's my son.''

Caralie wanted to slam her palms against her ears, slap a hand across Margaret's mouth, do anything to stop her from talking about Riley and love. She didn't want to hear it; knew that in this, Margaret was vastly mistaken. She had to be mistaken.

"I know Riley, and I've only seen him in love once before...and losing that love nearly destroyed him."

"Angela," Caralie said.

Margaret nodded. "When Angela died, I thought I'd lose my son as well. Kaycee was like a guardian angel sent to put him back on the course of the living. When Riley mentions your name I see a greater kind of love shining in his eyes than what he had before, and I'm desperately afraid for him." Margaret waved her hands once again. "I shouldn't be telling you this, but I have a favor to ask you."

"What?" Caralie asked, wishing she could run back to her car, and not have heard anything Margaret had said.

"When you break his heart, break it kindly."

Caralie opened her mouth, unsure what she intended to say, but in any case wasn't given the chance to reply as a knock sounded lightly on the door.

Margaret jumped up and drew the curtain aside just enough to give her a view of whoever stood outside. "It's Riley," she said as she unlocked the door to allow him entry.

"There's my girl." Margaret took Kaycee from his arms. The little girl smiled at Caralie as if delighted to see her.

"How did it go?" Margaret asked her son.

"It went." Riley looked from his mother to Caralie, his gaze shadowed and haunted. "We should have the results in a couple of weeks. I told the people at the lab to mail them to me."

Surely Margaret was mistaken, Caralie thought as she looked at him. Mothers often believed they knew what was in their child's heart, but that didn't always make it so. Caralie didn't want Riley to love her. Caralie had learned all about love. It didn't last. Love always walked away, left you abandoned...alone. Margaret had to be mistaken.

"We've got to go," he said to Caralie. "I set up a meeting with Stanley. We're to meet him in thirty minutes at the Coral Reef Restaurant."

Caralie was relieved that Riley's gaze held no intimate secrets, nothing but a matter-of-factness that eased her concerns. "Okay, I'm ready whenever you are."

She stood and smiled at Margaret, then gave Kaycee a quick hug.

"Mom, don't answer the door for anyone you don't recognize," Riley instructed. "And if you sense anything wrong, call the police."

"We'll be fine here," Margaret replied. "You just do what you have to do to get this mess cleared up." She touched her son's cheek lightly. "And be safe." She nodded to Caralie, then Riley and Caralie left.

"What about my car?" Caralie asked as Riley led her to his rental.

"Leave it. We'll pick it up later," he said.

Caralie looked back at the motel unit. "You think they'll be safe there?"

He nodded. "I've got an old friend of mine watching the place just to make sure. They should be all right.''

He was silent during the drive to the restaurant, distant in a way Caralie found almost comforting. Again she told herself Margaret was wrong. She'd apparently sensed the physical attraction that existed between her son and Caralie and had somehow mistaken that for love.

''Did you tell Stanley what the plan was?'' she asked.

''Not really. I just told him we had a hot story that involved the mayor. When I hung up he was salivating and begging for details.''

''This could all be dangerous, couldn't it?'' Caralie asked.

Riley shot her a sideways glance. ''If he killed your sister, then there's every reason to believe he might kill again. Sure, it might be dangerous. It's not too late to call it off if you're having second thoughts.''

''I'm having second, third and fourth,'' she said dryly. ''But I don't want to call anything off. I want him to pay—not just for her death, but for exploiting her weaknesses, abusing her love.'' She sat up straighter in the seat and drew a deep breath. ''I need to confront him. I need to look into his eyes when I tell him that I know what he did.''

Riley pulled into a parking space in front of the restaurant, shut off the engine, then turned to her. ''You're a strong woman, Caralie.'' He flashed her a look of admiration, then swallowed visibly. ''You'll make a good mother for Kaycee.''

"Just as you are a good father." She said the words softly, saw them arrow directly into his heart. "Riley, I'm not doing anything about the custody until we get those results back. If it turns out that you really are Kaycee's biological father, then I won't pursue the custody issue."

The instant the words left her mouth, she knew the rightness of them. Kaycee belonged with Riley. The little girl's best interests were served by keeping her with the man who loved her—the man who had bonded with her in the first days of her life.

Riley closed his eyes for a moment, as if he'd been handed a gift too enormous to comprehend. "But what about Loretta's request?" he asked, his voice filled with suppressed emotion.

Caralie frowned thoughtfully. "I can't know what was in Loretta's head when she wrote me that letter. Maybe she thought Monroe might be Kaycee's father and she didn't want him to have custody. Or maybe she just couldn't imagine what a wonderful father you would make. I promise if the DNA test shows that Monroe is her father and I get custody, I'll make sure you always play a major role in Kaycee's life."

Riley's dark eyes glittered unnaturally bright. He reached out and gently touched Caralie's cheek. And in his gaze, Caralie saw what Margaret had seen. Love. Radiating from him, shining in his eyes.

There was no mistaking the emotion and Caralie quickly looked away, focused on unfastening her seat belt. "We'd better get inside," she murmured, needing to escape before he spoke of his feelings; before she had to face and reject his love.

''YES, I'D LIKE TO SPEAK to Mayor Monroe,'' Caralie said into the pay phone outside the restaurant. Riley and Stanley had hashed out a plan to expose the mayor; this phone call was merely the first step.

''I'm sorry, Mayor Monroe isn't available right now,'' the receptionist replied.

''Could you leave him a message, please?'' Caralie twisted the cord around her fingers nervously. ''Tell him that Loretta's sister called and that curiosity doesn't always kill the cat...sometimes curiosity yields vital information. I'll be at this number if he decides to call me back.'' She reeled off the seven digits from the pay phone, then hung up. ''Now what?'' she asked the two men who stood nearby.

''Now we wait and see if he swallows the bait,'' Riley said.

They waited seven minutes and the pay phone rang. Riley nodded encouragingly and Caralie answered, her palm slick with sweat despite the cool afternoon air.

''Ms. Tracey.'' Michael Monroe's voice oozed across the line. ''Quite a cryptic message you left for me. I'm not sure I understand what it means.''

''Oh, you understand perfectly well,'' she retorted, his suave tones filling her with rage. ''I know everything, Mr. Monroe—everything about you and my sister.''

''I'm afraid I don't know what you're talking about—''

''You know exactly what I'm talking about,'' Caralie interrupted. Silence met her words—a long, pregnant silence.

"So, what do you want?" he finally asked.

"Meet me in two hours at dock thirteen. We'll talk then about what I want." She hung up before he could say anything more.

Instantly Riley's arms surrounded her. "You did terrific," he said as she trembled with emotion. "Stay strong for just a little while longer."

"Don't worry. We're going to get the bastard." Stanley beamed at Caralie, like a kid handed a coveted piece of candy. He looked at his watch. "Okay. I've got to get things set up. I'll meet you two at the dock in an hour."

"Do you think Monroe will really show up?" Caralie asked a few minutes later as she and Riley drove toward the assigned meeting place.

"He'll show. He can't afford not to. He doesn't know exactly what you know, what proof you might have."

"It would be so much easier if we could just go to the police."

Riley nodded. "But you know Paula was right. Michael Monroe owns the police department. We can't take a chance."

Caralie stared out the passenger-side window. It was all coming to an end. Her mission to solve the mystery of Loretta's death had been accomplished and it would be time for her to get on with her life—alone.

Marrying David was no longer an option and there was a fifty-fifty chance that when she left, she would go without Kaycee. And in walking away from Riley, she would leave a piece of her heart. But she'd been alone for most of her life; she did "alone" quite well.

Of course, there was a possibility that Riley wasn't Kaycee's biological father, and if that was the case, then Caralie would take custody, but she had meant what she'd told Riley; she would always make sure he was a big part of Kaycee's life.

She wanted him there for all the important moments that comprised a child's life. She wanted to see his face when Kaycee took her first step, when she enjoyed her first Easter-egg hunt, made her first valentine, experienced her first day of school. She wanted Kaycee to grow up knowing the very special man who loved her with all his heart.

And if the DNA tests proved Riley to be Kaycee's father, then Caralie wasn't sure what she would do. She desperately wanted the little girl in her own life, but agonized over the thought of depriving Riley.

However, one thing was certain: Before she made a final decision concerning Kaycee, before she got on with her life, she had to bring down Michael Monroe. She had to make her sister's murderer pay.

THE DOCK AREA SWARMED with workers. Riley parked his car and together he and Caralie walked toward dock thirteen. It had been Stanley who had suggested this particular spot, knowing it was presently not a working dock.

Dock thirteen was indeed deserted, the huge warehouse nearby empty. Unused barrels and cargo bins littered the area, providing plenty of hiding places. Riley assessed the location and found a huge bin where they could hide and observe any foot traffic that came into the area.

He wanted no surprises. That was why they had come directly to the dock. He hadn't wanted to give Michael Monroe time to get there first and orchestrate a setup that would result in harm to himself or Caralie.

He pulled Caralie into the dark confines of the walk-in metal container. ''We'll wait here for Stanley,'' he said, his voice echoing off the walls of the structure.

Caralie's tension radiated from her and he knew what she felt was both fear and anticipation. He hadn't exaggerated when he'd told her he admired her inner strength. She was not only strong enough to face a murderer, she was also strong enough to possibly make the choice to give him Kaycee, should he prove to be the biological father.

Riley felt the thick press of emotion clogging his throat. *Please...please let me be her father,* he prayed. Not because it mattered in the least to him, but because if he was proved the father, then Caralie would allow him to retain custody without a battle.

Of course, there was another way he could get to raise Kaycee—he and Caralie could raise her together, as man and wife. He loved Caralie, and he knew there was no way he intended to let her walk out of his life without at least telling her how he felt.

But now was not the time. He didn't want to speak

of love while standing in a smelly old bin waiting for a meeting with a murderer.

"You doing okay?" he asked.

She nodded, her eyes glowing in the semidarkness. "I just want this to be over, and I keep thinking of all the things that could go wrong. What if Stanley doesn't get here in time?"

"Trust me, nothing short of death will keep Stanley away," Riley said with a wry grin. "This is too big a story for him not to show."

Caralie released a tremulous sigh. "'A big story.' In the end that's all Loretta's life will count for."

"No, that isn't all," Riley said gently. "She left behind a legacy of love in one beautiful little girl." Caralie's eyes sparkled with tears and Riley placed an arm around her shoulder in comfort. The scent of her hair tantalized him, and the feel of her against him caused a protective surge inside him.

He thought of those moments when he'd made love to her, when their bodies had fit so perfectly together and moved in sweet unison. He remembered the times they'd laughed, the comfortable give-and-take between them.

He was suddenly afraid. Fear rippled through Wild Man Riley. He'd been in hundreds of dangerous situations in the past but never had he felt so afraid. He didn't fear for himself, but he feared for her. They had no idea how dangerous Michael Monroe might be; had no clue what the man was capable of.

"I shouldn't have let you do this," he said.

She stepped back from him, her eyes huge and

luminous. "There's no way you could have stopped me. This is something I have to do."

"Caralie..." Riley's love for her bubbled up inside him, begging to be released. He needed to tell her of his love, wanted to ask her to spend her life with him. But at that moment Stanley came into view and Riley lost his chance to speak of what was in his heart.

Later, he promised himself. He only hoped he got an opportunity to tell her later.

Chapter Fourteen

An early dusk seeped across the sky, the approaching night casting long shadows as Michael Monroe and his two minions came into view.

Caralie stared at the mayor unflinchingly as he and his goons approached where she and Riley stood. Riley felt the strength radiating from her as she faced the man who'd killed her sister.

Michael Monroe carried himself with the grace and arrogance of a man accustomed to commanding attention and respect. His two burly bodyguards walked slightly behind him, as if in deference to his greatness.

''Ms. Tracey and Mr. Kincaid. I'm not sure why you called this meeting. I'm afraid there must be some sort of a misunderstanding,'' he began.

''There's no misunderstanding,'' Caralie replied, her features reflecting her distaste for him and his pretended ignorance. ''There's no point in lying. We know you had an affair with my sister.''

''That's ridiculous,'' he scoffed. ''Your poor sister was deluded. While working on my campaign she developed an unhealthy obsession with me. Ask Bob, here—he's my campaign manager.'' He gestured toward the big, square-jawed man beside him.

Bob nodded, his pale eyes revealing no emotion. ''She was crazy. More than once I had to have security remove her from the premises of the campaign headquarters.''

''You're a liar. Both of you are liars,'' Riley said angrily. He eyed Michael Monroe. ''You put Loretta up in that expensive apartment. You paid her rent, paid her bills.''

Michael smirked. ''You have no proof of that.''

''You made sure of that, didn't you? What did you do, sneak into the apartment and take away any physical evidence that might tie you to her?'' Riley clenched his fists at his sides.

''But we do have proof,'' Caralie said. ''We have a baby. What would DNA tests show about Loretta's little girl and you?''

Michael's face blanched slightly. ''That proves nothing.'' He drew a deep breath and held his hands out in a gesture of defeat. ''Okay...I'll admit I was weak. My wife and I were having some problems and I had a one-night stand with your sister.''

''It was no one-night stand. You had a long-term affair and when she pressed you to divorce your wife and marry her, you killed her!'' Caralie accused. Riley could see tears spring to her eyes and he longed to take her hurt from her, wished he could suffer it instead.

''Whoa...slow down...wait a minute.'' Michael held up his hands. ''I didn't kill anyone. If you're talking about that fire at the hospital in Galveston, I had nothing at all to do with that. You aren't going to try to pin a murder on me."

Caralie faltered. Riley hesitated as well, recognizing a ring of truth in the vehemence of his tone. "Then you had somebody set the fire..." Caralie began.

"No way." Michael shook his head, looking first at Caralie, then at Riley. "Look, I'll admit that Loretta and I had an affair. She was attractive, sexy, and exciting as hell. For a while it was great, but she grew more and more demanding." He raked a hand through his hair, leaving the neatly styled strands standing on end. "We had a good thing going, then she had to go crazy and start nagging at me to divorce my wife, marry her. When she got pregnant, I told her that was it—nobody was going to trap me into doing something stupid."

"And so you threatened her, wrote notes telling her to keep her mouth shut," Caralie added flatly.

"Yeah, I did do that. I told her she could stay in the apartment rent-free until the kid was born, then I'd give her twenty-five thousand dollars to disappear from my life for good. She agreed. Hell, the money should still be in an account at the First National Bank. All she had to do was keep her mouth shut."

Riley saw the all-consuming rage seep away from Caralie, leaving behind a weary confusion. "But you tried to kill us..." she whispered.

Square-jawed Bob laughed mirthlessly. "If we'd wanted to kill you, you'd be dead. It was a game of threats, a calculated effort to make you two go away and stop asking questions."

Riley knew that what the man said was true. He

now recognized that there had been a hundred ways, a hundred times when he and Caralie might have been killed. It had been a game of bluff, with no discernible winner so far.

"We aren't going away," Caralie said softly. "You used my sister, played with her emotions and exploited her need to be loved. I think the voters need to know just what kind of man you are."

Caralie screamed as in one swift motion Bob pulled a gun from his jacket and yanked her against him. Riley tensed to spring, but stopped as Bob cocked the weapon at Caralie's temple. "Do you really think I'm going to let you two ruin everything we've worked for? Michael's going to the top. He'll be President one day."

"Bob, let her go," Michael commanded, his voice ringing with authority.

"Hey, Bob, what are you doing?" The other bodyguard started to pull a gun from his jacket.

"Don't do it, Sam!" Bob screamed. "I'll kill you if you get in my way!"

Sam dropped his hand.

Riley died a thousand deaths as he saw the terror in Caralie's eyes, recognized his own helplessness in coming to her aid. "For God's sake, man," he said. "Let her go. This won't solve anything."

"I'll shut her up and then I'll shut you up," Bob yelled, a crazed light in his eyes. He took several steps backward, dragging Caralie with him. "I can't let you screw things up. I've worked too hard for Michael."

"Right now all he's facing is a charge of moral weakness, but if you do anything stupid, you'll destroy any hope of any career for Michael in the future,'' Riley told him.

''Come on, Bob. Be reasonable,'' Sam added, his features taut with fear.

''It's too late. Don't you understand that? I started that fire. I had to stop that woman from ruining Michael's career.''

''Oh, Bob.'' Michael sagged visibly, then straightened once again. ''Listen to me...put the gun down and let her go.'' Michael held his hands out pleadingly, his voice strained. ''We'll work this out somehow. We'll fix things for you.''

''Michael, we can fix things right now,'' Bob said with a renewed urgency. ''We kill them all, then nobody knows and we're home free.''

''Somebody will know,'' Riley countered. He yanked open his shirt and pulled at a wire taped to his chest. ''Someplace around here there's a reporter, and he has every word on tape.''

''No.'' Bob's gaze darted around the area at the same time the barrel of the gun wavered away from Caralie's head.

Riley exploded into action. He grabbed Bob's weapon, forcing the big men's hand into the air. At the same time he shoved Caralie away, vaguely aware of her grunt of pain as she fell to the dock.

For a long moment Riley and Bob struggled for the gun, Riley trying to rip the weapon from Bob's grip, and Bob attempting to aim it at Riley.

Bob fought with the strength of a madman, but Riley fought with the knowledge that he was not only battling for his own life, but more important, for Caralie's.

With a cry born of desperation, he drew on every ounce of his physical strength and shoved at his opponent.

Bob fell backward, pulling the trigger as he went down. A piercing crack resounded, followed by a second one. As he hit the ground the gun skittered out of his hand and out of reach.

Riley saw Caralie scramble for the weapon at the same time the wail of sirens sounded in the air. He held on to Bob, who kicked and clawed, punched and grabbed in an effort to escape.

Michael and the other bodyguard made no move to help Riley. They stood perfectly still beneath the spell of the trembling woman who held a gun pointed at them.

Riley roared in pain as one of Bob's kicks connected with the underside of his chin. Blood spurted from the reopened wound, the sight of it renewing Riley's vigor.

With a right cross he snapped Bob's head back and it thudded harshly against the ground. Eyes rolling back, Bob fell unconscious just as a bevy of patrolmen came running toward them.

''Drop the gun!'' One of them shouted, falling into a firing position, his weapon trained on Caralie.

''Hold your fire!'' Michael yelled back. He turned to Caralie. ''I swear I didn't know. I didn't know he set the fire.''

Caralie's hand shook and a trickle of sweat made its way down the side of her face. Still, she pointed the gun at the mayor. ''All she wanted was for somebody to love her.'' Caralie's voice trembled with emotion. "She just wanted somebody to be there for her. She shouldn't have had to die for that."

"I swear, I didn't know," Michael repeated, his eyes wide with fear.

"Caralie." Riley spoke her name softly, seeing the utter terror coupled with the rage that darkened her eyes. Her hand shook and he knew how much she wanted to pull the trigger, shoot the man who had been inadvertently responsible for her sister's death. "Caralie...honey...drop the gun. It's over."

For another long moment she held the gun pointed at Michael, an obvious internal battle being waged. Her lower lip trembled and with a deep, wrenching sob, she threw down the weapon and raced for Riley's arms. As Riley held her, Michael gestured for the officers to handcuff Bob and take him with them.

"Monroe," Riley called after him as he started to walk away. "We lied about the kid. We had the tests run. You aren't the father. I am."

Michael nodded wearily and Riley felt no guilt over his lie. Caralie's arms tightened around his waist, as if in silent support of the blatant deception.

Riley held Caralie until all the police were gone and night had fallen around them. They didn't speak. There were no words. The questions about Loretta's death had been answered.

How sad, Riley thought, that her life had been sacrificed by an ambitious campaign manager, that she'd died for a political career.

Stanley had hurried off moments before, burning with the fervor to put words on paper. The tape he possessed would be instrumental in sending Bob to prison and destroying any political hope, Michael Monroe might have had for the future.

Riley had requested only one thing of his friend—that in the articles he wrote he made no mention of Kaycee. Riley didn't want the little girl tied to the scandal that would ensue. It was far too big a burden for a child to carry.

"Come on. Let's go get Kaycee and go home," Riley finally said to Caralie, who had her head burrowed against his chest.

She nodded and released her hold on him. Hand in hand they walked back to his car. Caralie was silent on the way to the motel. Riley sensed she was doing her final grieving for her sister and didn't want to intrude. When they arrived, even Kaycee's presence couldn't seem to pull Caralie out of her silent reverie.

After they'd taken Margaret home and returned to the house, Caralie disappeared into her bedroom while Kaycee demanded Riley's attention in building a tower of blocks.

She squealed in delight as their tower grew and Riley's heart constricted painfully at the sight of her childish joy.

Was he going to lose her? He knew that if the test results showed him not to be the biological father, Caralie would still make sure he got plenty of visitation with Kaycee. But it wouldn't be the same. He would miss so many moments in her development, so many events that happened only once.

All the heartbreak of sharing Kaycee could be circumvented in a very simple way. If he and Caralie built a life together, then Kaycee would be raised in the stability of a two-parent home, a home filled with passion and love, with laughter and respect.

He realized he had to tell Caralie he loved her. He had to tell her this instant. With an urgency he'd never felt before, he picked up Kaycee and placed her in her playpen. Ignoring the little girl's indignant cry of protest, Riley went down the hallway and knocked on Caralie's door. "Yes...come in."

He opened the door and stopped, his heart clutching as he saw her open suitcase on the bed. "What are you doing?" he asked.

"Packing." She turned to the closet and pulled out a handful of clothes. "It's over, Riley. I learned what I needed to know about Loretta's death and now it's time for me to leave." She didn't look at him. She focused all her concentration on meticulously folding a blouse.

"But I told you that it wasn't necessary for you to leave right away." Riley's heart pounded in his ears. "Caralie...I don't want you to leave."

Her gaze, startled and wide, shot to his. "I have to, Riley. I told you that when I found out what had happened to Loretta, I intended to get on with my life."

"Why can't your life be here? With me?" The words tumbled out of him, as if a dam had burst and no longer held back his emotions. "We can build a life together, you and me and Kaycee. I love you, Caralie."

He wasn't sure what he'd expected. He'd hoped for a joyous reaction from her. He'd hoped she'd fall into his arms and proclaim her love for him, promise him love forever. He hadn't expected the grimace of pain that crossed her face.

She placed the blouse in her suitcase, then looked back at him, her eyes dark and turbulent. "That would certainly solve things with Kaycee, wouldn't it?"

"That's not what this is about." Riley approached her. He'd been afraid that was what she would think, and knew he had to make her understand his love for her had nothing to do with Kaycee.

No matter what happened with his daughter, he would always love Caralie. He placed his hands on her shoulders, felt her tension. "Caralie, this is about me—and you. This is about the fact that I love you more than I've ever loved a woman before in my life."

She closed her eyes, as if his words caused her enormous pain. "Riley...don't."

"Don't what?" He stroked a finger down the side of her cheek. "Don't love you? It's too late. I do and nothing is going to change that fact."

She stepped away from him and grabbed another blouse from the closet. As she folded the silky material, he thought he saw the sparkle of tears dampening her long eyelashes.

"Caralie, talk to me. I want you to marry me, to spend the rest of your life with me." Riley's voice held all the love, all the emotion that he'd kept inside for so long. He wanted to take her in his arms, hold her, make love to her for an eternity.

"Riley...I can't marry you." In her eyes was the same emotional distance he'd seen after they'd made love.

All of Riley's hopes, all his dreams whooshed out of him in a sigh. "Is this about David? I know you said at one time you intended to marry him, but I thought when you and I..." His voice trailed off as she shook her head.

"No, this isn't about David. I realized the first time you and I made love that I didn't love David and couldn't marry him."

"But you do love me." Riley once again moved closer to her. He saw the evidence of his conviction shining in her eyes. It was there for only a moment, then was swallowed by forced dispassion. "I know you love me, Caralie. It shows in the way you kiss me, in the way you move with me when we make love."

Again he reached up and stroked her face. "I see it in your eyes...feel it coming from your heart." He touched her lips softly, gently with the tip of his finger. "If it isn't true, then tell me I'm wrong."

"I can't." The words seeped from her with regret. "I can't tell you you're wrong." Riley's heart soared. "But I won't marry you."

Once again, tears glittered like diamonds on her lashes, framing eyes the color of deep regret. "I intend to live my life alone. If Kaycee isn't biologically your child, then I'll raise her and she and I will build a life together. But I don't want a man in my life. I won't...I can't...depend on love." She moved away from him and placed the blouse in the suitcase, then went to the closet for more clothing.

Riley's heart plummeted to the pit of his stomach at the look of steely resolve he'd seen on her face.

She loved him, but intended to turn her back on that love.

It made no sense. How could she love him, know he loved her and yet deny them a future together? As he watched, she continued to pack her suitcase. She finished emptying the closet, then moved to one of the dresser drawers and began unloading those clothes into the suitcase.

Riley's mind whirled, as he tried to understand what was going on with her, why she would turn her back on him. On love.

"All along, you've been talking about how wounded Loretta was from your childhood." His tone was gentle, thoughtful, as he voiced the realization that now filled his head. "But in truth, you're far more wounded than she ever was. At least she didn't give up. She spent her short life looking to fill the void left inside her."

"And look what it got her," Caralie retorted as she slammed her suitcase closed.

The heat of frustrated anger swept over Riley. "You were willing to face her murderer, put your very life at risk, but you're scared to love," he accused.

"Great passion always leads to great pain."

He stared at her. "Is that really what you believe? Don't you see that no passion leads to no life?"

"I'll have a life," she protested. She picked up the suitcase and moved past him, out into the hallway. "I don't need a man to make me whole. I don't need anyone."

"Oh, honey, this isn't about need. You're right. No woman absolutely needs a man to complete her, but having love enhances your life. It's a choice you make, a choice to share life, to share the good and the bad with somebody.''

Riley followed her into the living room, where Kaycee clapped her hands in glee at their appearance. ''Don't turn your back on love. For God's sake, don't turn your back on *my* love,'' he said, desperate to break through the walls of her self-protection.

She didn't look at him, nor did she reply. She set the suitcase down and went to the playpen and lifted Kaycee into her arms. She buried her face in the hollow of Kaycee's neck. And Kaycee hugged her, her chubby hand patting her back as if the little girl sensed the tumultuous emotion in the air.

Giving Kaycee a kiss, Caralie then placed her in the playpen again and picked up her suitcase. Her shoulders were stiff with resolve and her eyes were dry and solemn. ''I'm sorry, Riley.'' She moved toward the front door and he fought the impulse to run to her, grab her into his arms and hold her until she changed her mind.

''You'll let me know when you get the test results?''

He nodded numbly.

''I'll get a room at the Lone Star Motel.'' With those words, she walked out the door and out of his life.

Chapter Fifteen

He loves me.

Riley's words of love haunted Caralie as she drove away from his house and toward the familiar motel. Her heart ached with the burden of his love. She hadn't wanted him to love her, had never intended to do anything but settle the issue of Kaycee's custody and solve the mystery of Loretta's death.

She loved him, too. But she knew love wasn't for her. She'd taken that route, had watched too many people walk out of her life—first her mother, then a succession of foster parents. But Riley was wrong about her being wounded. She wasn't denying herself his love out of fear; she was reacting with a strong sense of reality.

Caralie tightened her grip on the steering wheel. She wasn't wounded…and she wasn't afraid. She was just too smart to count on love.

There were some people born to find love, and others who were born to be alone. She was one of the latter. She refused to be dependent on any man, refused to give her heart only to have it broken someplace down the line. It wasn't a matter of being afraid; it was a matter of being smart.

Within minutes she'd checked into the same room she'd stayed in when she'd first arrived in town. There was little comfort in the familiarity of the gold-corded bedspread and the serene landscape painting on the wall.

Emotionally, her heart cried out to be with Riley, snuggled in his king-size bed, his warm skin the only blanket she needed. But she couldn't allow emotions to rule her. That was how her mother had been, how Loretta had lived her life.

Besides, despite his protests to the contrary, Caralie knew the issue of Kaycee was all tied together with Riley's love. Somehow he'd managed to convince himself he was in love with Caralie because it solved the custody problem. If he took Caralie, then he wouldn't have to lose Kaycee.

Caralie shed her clothes and pulled on her nightgown, hoping that a good night's sleep would dull the aching vividness of Riley's features, would blur the memory of his touch on her face as he'd spoken of his love for her.

He'd forget about her. In time, he'd forget he ever believed he loved her. They'd see each other when they transferred Kaycee back and forth for visits, and eventually they would become two pleasant strangers who'd shared moments of passion in another lifetime.

She closed her eyes against her burning tears, wondering why on earth her good, practical decision to turn her back on the love Riley offered should make her cry. She desperately sought the oblivion of sleep, but instead found only the wrenching grief and anguish of heartbreak.

During the next ten days time alternately flew and crawled by. Caralie spent much of those days in front of her motel-room television, watching the news bulletins that chronicled Michael Monroe's descent from public favor and the arrest of Bob Johnson, his campaign manager, for arson and murder.

Stanley had his fifteen minutes of fame, being interviewed by a local newscaster about the tape he'd made—a tape that wouldn't be entered into evidence in the case, but made great listening excitement for viewers. And Stanley remained true to his promise to Riley; Kaycee wasn't mentioned in any of the newscasts or stories carried in the papers.

Every afternoon, Caralie went to Riley's house and took Kaycee for a walk in her stroller. Riley kept his distance, maintaining a businesslike attitude that broke Caralie's heart and yet made things easier.

She felt as if she were in limbo, awaiting the test results that would possibly change her life forever. She spent one day putting applications in at the local hospitals and nursing homes, hoping for a position as a nurse's aide. Eventually she'd need to rent an apartment, but had decided to wait to find a permanent place until the issue of where Kaycee was going to live was settled.

Riley had called her earlier that morning and asked her to meet him and Kaycee at a park near his house for a picnic. Although she knew it would be an exercise in torture to spend any time in his company and try not to fall more deeply in love with him, she couldn't deny herself the pleasure in spite of the pain.

As she drove toward the park, she rolled down the car window, allowing in the unseasonably warm breeze. Sweatshirt weather in January. Caralie drew in a deep breath of the sweet, fresh air.

She pulled into the gravel parking area of the neighborhood refuge and turned off the engine. Immediately she spied Riley and Kaycee. She smiled, her heart expanding at the picture of father and daughter. Riley sat on a swing, his broad shoulders squeezed between the two chains that held the wooden seat. On his lap Kaycee was a pink bundle of happiness as they swayed back and forth.

While Caralie watched, Riley bent his head down and kissed Kaycee's cheek. The little girl reached up to lovingly pat his face. And in that instant, Caralie knew she would be wrong to try to take Kaycee away from him. No matter what the results of the DNA tests, Kaycee belonged with Riley.

The knowledge sent a shaft of pain through her like an arrow ripping through flesh to her heart. She realized that the best interests of Kaycee were served by her remaining with the father who loved her so.

There was no way to know for sure what had been in Loretta's mind when she'd written the letter to Caralie asking her to take custody. However, Caralie knew one thing for certain: Loretta would want her child to be surrounded by love, and that was what Riley gave to Kaycee.

Caralie would have a special place in Kaycee's life, but it would be that of aunt rather than surrogate mother. Although this decision caused her heart to ache, she knew it was the right choice—the best choice for the niece she loved.

And in settling the decision about Kaycee, Caralie knew she would also be giving Riley back his heart. Without the custody issue to muddy the waters, Riley would realize he'd never really loved Caralie.

Riley spied her as she got out of her car. He waved to her as she approached the swing set, her heart heavy but buoyed with a sense of rightness.

''Hi,'' he greeted her with a tentative smile.

''Hi, yourself,'' she returned as she sat down on the swing next to them. Kaycee smiled and cooed nonsensical words, as if trying to tell Caralie all about her day so far.

''It's a perfect day for a picnic,'' he said as their swings set to gliding in a matching rhythm. ''I'm glad you came.''

She looked away, finding him achingly attractive with his dark, windblown hair and ruddy cheeks. ''I couldn't very well miss Kaycee's first official picnic.''

''It wouldn't have been the same without you here.''

Caralie turned to look at him, the softness of his gaze, the sweetness in his voice stabbing through her. ''I'm sure Kaycee would have a good time with or without my presence,'' she said, refusing to be drawn into his seduction.

''No, she told me she's glad you came.''

''She's talking in full sentences now?'' Caralie asked as she looked back at him. ''I knew she was bright, but I didn't realize how bright.''

He chuckled—the deep, melodic sound warming Caralie. ''She's the brightest kid in the world and even though she didn't actually say the words, I felt her excitement when she saw you. I've got a blanket spread out over there.'' He pointed to the shady area beneath a tree next to a barbecue grill. ''Why don't we move over there and I'll get the fire started.''

As Riley lit the charcoal, Caralie played with Kaycee. ''It will take a few minutes for this to be ready to cook the hot dogs,'' he said as he flopped down on the blanket next to Caralie.

She shifted positions in an attempt to gain a little distance from him. The scent of his cologne wafted over her, reminding her of the touch of his hand against her skin, the heat of his lips plying hers, the utter completeness she'd felt as their bodies had moved as one.

Damn him. Why did he have to be so attractive? Why did she have to want him so?

''I assume you've seen all the news stories,'' he said as he grabbed one of Kaycee's blocks and added it to the top of the tower she'd started to build.

''Yes.''

''I have a feeling Michael Monroe will never attempt to run for public office again.''

Caralie smiled cynically. ''Oh, I don't know. Politicians have a way of rising from the ashes of disgrace.'' She sighed. ''At least Bob Johnson is being charged and will serve time. There's comfort in that.''

Riley reached out and touched her cheek. ''Have you found the peace you needed?''

She nodded, fighting the desire to lean into his touch, move closer against the heat and safety his body offered. She loved him, and she feared that love. She wanted him, but knew she had to deny herself in order to keep her heart secure.

"What about you?" she asked, edging still farther away from him on the blanket. "Are you back at work in your studio?"

His gaze hardened somewhat, letting her know he was aware of her subtle physical distancing. "Had a sitting yesterday—a couple celebrating their fiftieth wedding anniversary." He opened one of the bags beside him and pulled out a large envelope. "I brought you a present."

"A present?" She took the envelope from him and opened it. She gasped in surprise as she pulled out the photos inside, the pictures he'd taken of her on New Year's Eve.

She looked at each one, her cheeks flaming bright as she remembered how they had made love that same night. He'd managed to capture her desire for him. It was in her eyes and in her body language in each and every pose.

"They're very good," she said, her voice sounding husky to her own ears. "Thank you."

"I also got something else today." He reached back into the bag and withdrew another envelope. "The test results." He stared at the envelope for a long moment. "I haven't opened it yet." He looked at Caralie, his gaze intent. "I've said it before, but I need to say it again. I don't give a damn what these results indicate. I'm Kaycee's father and nothing is ever going to change that."

"Riley..." She reached out and closed her hand over his hand that held the envelope. "There's no reason for you to open that. There's no reason for you to know the results.''

He frowned, obviously confused by her words. ''But then how will we settle the custody issue?''

Caralie swallowed hard. ''It's settled. I won't fight you for custody.''

He stared at her as if she'd suddenly spoken a foreign language. ''What are you talking about?''

She removed her hand from his. ''Oh, Riley, Kaycee belongs with you. It would be wrong for me to take her from you. I'd like to be a part of her life, but it's right that she remain with you.''

He closed his eyes, but not before she saw the mist of grateful tears. She felt the burn of her own tears, but knew that what she was doing was right.

He swallowed hard and looked at her. ''Are you sure?'' he asked, his voice a mere whisper. ''Are you really sure?''

''I've never been so sure of anything in my life. I've done nothing but think about it all week.'' Caralie looked at Kaycee, who'd discarded the blocks and now played with large plastic shapes of farm animals. ''I realized on the way here that I've been clinging to Kaycee because she's all that's left of my family. I haven't been thinking of her welfare. I've been selfishly thinking that she'll fill up the empty spaces in my life—and that's too big a burden for a little girl.''

''But it's not too big a burden for me,'' Riley replied. He scooted closer to her, the envelope containing the test results falling to the ground at his side. ''Caralie, I appreciate the fact that you don't intend to fight for custody of Kaycee...but it isn't enough.''

''What do you mean?'' she asked, his nearness causing her heart to thud unnaturally fast.

''I want it all. I want Kaycee *and* you.''

''Riley, that's not necessary. There's no reason for you to say that now.''

He grabbed her by the shoulders, his eyes alive with a fire that warmed her to her soul. ''Don't you understand, Caralie? I love you. This has nothing to do with Kaycee. It has never had anything to do with Kaycee. Since you left, my house doesn't feel like a home. It's empty and lacks life. It needs you. *I* need you.''

''Please stop.'' She jerked away from him and stood, her back turned toward him as tears streamed down her face. ''Don't you understand? I love you, but I'm afraid. You were right the other day when you told me I was wounded. I'm wounded and scared. I don't want to love you. I don't want to need you.''

''Caralie...let me show you something.'' His voice was calm, measured. She turned around and watched him help Kaycee to her feet. ''Come on, sweetie. Let's show off a little bit.'' He helped her balance, then backed away from her.

Emitting a squeal of excitement, Kaycee took one step...two steps...then plunged forward, her arms reaching for Riley, who caught her before she could fall.

''Oh, that's wonderful!'' Caralie exclaimed as Kaycee clapped her hands together and grinned at the two adults.

"It is, isn't it," Riley said. He walked over to where Caralie stood and framed her face with his palms on either side. "Amazing, isn't it...the desire for independence that teaches children to walk. But did you notice, when she felt herself starting to fall, she reached out—she needed somebody to be there to catch her."

Caralie gazed into his eyes—eyes so dark, yet with a piercing light that somehow penetrated the dark places inside her.

"We all need somebody, Caralie," he continued. "It's good to be independent and strong, but it's also nice to have somebody's arms hold you when you're feeling weak."

He frowned and with the tip of his index finger traced across her bottom lip. "I wish...I wish I could have known you years ago. I wish I had been there when your mother left you, when all those other people walked out of your life and you were afraid and alone. I would have held you so tight, loved you so much. I would have chased your fear and your loneliness away."

The words, so sweetly spoken, so earnestly meant, created a fissure in the protective shell around her heart. Tears burned and pressed behind her eyes as fear battled with desire, trepidation warred with ravenous need.

"I wish I had been there when you and Loretta were giving all your friends fairy-tale names. You would have called me Prince Charming. You would have known even then that I was the one who would love you forever." At those words, the last of the casing around her heart fell away, leaving her aching and vulnerable—and so much in love.

"Marry me, Caralie. Marry me and let's build a family together, you and me and Kaycee."

"Yes." The single word escaped her on a rush of adrenaline. "Yes, yes, yes!" She laughed, tears mingling with her joy.

His arms wrapped around her and his lips captured hers in a kiss that spoke of desire and love and "happily ever after."

"Ga-ga!" Kaycee yelled for attention.

Laughing, Caralie and Riley reached for the little girl. "There's just one thing left to do," Caralie said as Riley placed Kaycee on his hip.

"What's that?" he asked.

Caralie went to the edge of the blanket, where the envelope containing the test results lay on the ground. She picked it up and stepped over to the grill. "It was a fire that brought Kaycee to you as a daughter. I think it's poetic justice that it should be a fire that returns her to you as a daughter. For right now, that's all we need to know." Without waiting for a reply, she dropped the envelope onto the hot coals. Riley placed an arm around her as together they watched the envelope blacken and crinkle, then burst into flames. They watched silently until there was nothing left but ashes.

"And from the ashes, rose not a phoenix, but a family," Riley said. He kissed Kaycee's cheek, then pulled Caralie back into his arms. "I love you, Caralie, and I intend to spend the rest of my life showing you just how much."

A shiver raced up Caralie's spine as she saw the

fire of passion that lit his eyes. ‘‘I love you, Riley. Forever and always.’’

He smiled, his dimple flashing in his cheek. ‘‘I guess Stanley was right when he said you’d tamed Wild Man Riley.’’

Caralie laughed and shook her head. ‘‘No, it was Kaycee who tamed the wild man. I’m just the woman who loves him.’’

Again Riley’s eyes burned at a fever pitch. ‘‘Come on,’’ he said. ‘‘Let’s pack up and get you checked out of that motel. I want you home where you belong.’’

Caralie’s heart sang with joy at his words. Home. Home with Riley and Kaycee.

Home to a lifetime of love.

COMING NEXT MONTH

#501 A COWBOY'S HONOR by Laura Gordon
The Cowboy Code
Cameron McQuaid was both a cowboy and a lawman, and lived his life by a code of honor. Yet, when Frani Landon comes to town to catch a killer, Cameron finds his honor—and his heart—on the line.

#502 FAMILIAR VALENTINE by Caroline Burnes
Fear Familiar
A velvet Valentine's night, a threatening attacker—and suddenly, Celeste Levert found herself swept to safety in Dan Morgan's strong arms. He promised to keep her safe and secure, but couldn't offer his heart—until a black cat played Cupid....

#503 LAWMAN LOVER by Saranne Dawson
Michael Quinn's tenacity made him an extraordinary cop. It also made him an exceptional lover. And Amanda Sturdevant remembered everything, every caress and kiss, of her one night with him, but nothing of a long-ago night of terror that had left a woman dead and Amanda barely with her life—and amnesia....

#504 JACKSON'S WOMAN by Judi Lind
Her Protector
Everyone called her Verity McBride, but only Vera knew no one would believe the truth about her identity. But now with a murder charge hanging over her head, she turned to Jericho Jackson for help and found a love for all time—even though he thought she was someone else....